For Solo Voice

Susanna Tamaro was born in Trieste in
1957, and now lives in Rome. She studied
cinematography and made scientific
documentaries for RAI. Her first novel,
La testa fra le nuvole (*Head in the
Clouds*), appeared in 1989; *Per Voce Solo*
(*For Solo Voice*) was published in 1991;
and *Va' dove ti porta il cuore* (*Follow Your
Heart*) in 1994. She also writes for
children.

SUSANNA TAMARO

For Solo Voice

**Translated from the Italian by
SHARON WOOD**

Minerva

A Minerva Paperback
FOR SOLO VOICE

First published in Great Britain in 1995
by Carcanet Press Limited

This Minerva edition published 1997

Minerva
Random House 20 Vauxhall Bridge Road,
London SW1V 2SA

Random House Australia (Pty) Limited
20 Alfred Street, Milsons Point, Sydney
New South Wales 2061, Australia

Random House New Zealand Limited
18 Poland Road, Glenfield,
Auckland 10, New Zealand

Random House South Africa (Pty) Limited
Endulini, 5a Jubilee Road, Parktown 2193, South Africa

Random House UK Limited Reg. No. 954009

Originally published in Italian
under the titles *Per Voce Sola*
Copyright © 1991, Marsilio editori spa, Venice
Translation copyright © 1995 Sharon Wood

A CIP catalogue record for this title
is available from the British Library

ISBN 0 7493 8646 0

Phototypeset in Century Expanded
by Intype London Ltd
Printed and bound in Great Britain
by Cox & Wyman Ltd, Reading, Berkshire

For my grandmother,
Elsa

For years everything stayed down there, in an iron box so deeply buried within me that I never knew exactly what it contained. I knew I was carrying an unstable, inflammable cargo, more secret than sex and more dangerous than spectres and ghosts.

Helen Epstein,
Children of the Holocaust,
1979

Contents

Monday Again

Dear diary, Monday again. Today is the first real autumn day: it's windy and the leaves, yellow at last, are whirling in the air. Going by the calendar, autumn should have started some time ago but with these holes in the atmosphere we've got now you can't be sure of anything any more, not even the regular changing of the seasons. I wonder about that now and again. I'm thinking of little Dorrie, of course, not of me and Jeff. Speaking of Dorrie, it's six years to the day that she's been with us. It wasn't me who remembered but my assistant at the publisher's. When we went to the bar she insisted on getting me a glass of sparkling wine. It was only when she raised it and said 'Here's to your little puppy' that it came to me. Of course, the anniversary! A kind of second birthday. The day she was born and the day we adopted her. I remember so clearly how excited Jeff and I were. They didn't know when she was born, nor where. A night watchman had found her in a rubbish bin. She was white, of Hispanic origin maybe. But if she'd been black or yellow it would have been all the same. Ever since they confirmed we would never be able to have children of our own we'd wanted nothing else. As soon as we were outside the Institute Jeff hugged her in his arms and said, 'In the rubbish! It sounds like one of those fairy stories you publish!'

Yes, a fairy story! That's just what we were talking about at today's editorial meeting. We are launching a new series for children between six and ten years old. Laurie, my partner, reckons this is a good moment to bring out scary stories. She says that's what children want, monsters, witches, giants foaming at the mouth, wicked stepfathers who eat their children. I'm not in favour of all this, of course. I think we should be offering children nothing but the best, making them dream: they're so tender, fragile and with such vivid imaginations.

This evening Jeff and I went out to dinner. He took me to that little Italian place we used to go to when we were just married. He didn't mention Dorrie's anniversary, but I'm almost positive that's why he took me out, to celebrate it. He's so discreet, Jeff, so absolutely hypersensitive. As I'm about to drop off to sleep, I often wonder what my life would have been like without him. I can't picture it at all. Besides I'm happy as I am, so why should I want to know?

P.S. As we were going home I tripped on the stairs. I don't know how it happened but it must have been a funny sight, me rolling down like a sack of potatoes. Jeff was a bit worried, but I got up and said 'No harm done'. And we fell about laughing.

Dear diary, I was a bit over-optimistic yesterday about that fall. In fact this morning when I woke up I realized I ached all over. Then in the bathroom, when I looked in the mirror, came the real surprise. My eye was black and purple, a real shiner, like a boxer's.

Jeff wasn't there, he'd already gone out. His work demands so much of him that sometimes I don't know where he finds the energy to carry on!

Anyway, I decided not to go to the publisher's today. I'll have a nice day at home, with little Dorrie. It's pouring with rain and when she comes back from school we'll snuggle under the blankets and I'll tell her fairy stories until tea-time. She'll want Bluebeard or Tom Thumb as usual, and as usual I'll try and tell her the story of Cinderella. There is sometimes a shadow in the little girl's eyes which I don't like. With my stories, with gentle coaxing, I can get the better of it and make it go away.

It's ten in the evening now. The afternoon went according to plan. We stayed in bed watching the rain fall, telling stories. It was five o'clock before we got up. Dorrie had to write a little essay for tomorrow, on 'My Dad'. Even though writing normally comes so easily to her this time she looked at me bewildered, her pen suspended in the air over a blank piece of paper. So I helped her. I can well understand, I said, that you don't know what to write; Daddy is so wonderful that it's hard to know where to begin! So I suggested she write that he's a lawyer, that he always defends the poor, that he was a bit like Robin Hood; tall and strong, strong enough to strangle

3

an elephant with two fingers or to lift us both over the balcony railing without any bother, as if we were two pieces of paper. Dorrie stopped looking so puzzled, she began to write and wrote for a whole hour with absolute attention and concentration.

This evening Jeff didn't come home to dinner; there are times his work absorbs him to the point where he hasn't even got time to call me. Not that there was any dinner this evening. Jeff has decided we should start a new diet; every other evening, nothing but boiling water. A doctor from California invented it. He claims it purifies you, keeps your thoughts light. It's true, after a week I already feel better. With all the rubbish there is in the air and in what we eat, it's really important to give our insides the occasional spring-cleaning. Inner clarity, of body and soul. That's the idea. Little Dorrie made something of a fuss though. She wanted cornflakes and milk, not boiling water. I gently explained to her that Daddy knows what's good for us. She soon saw reason and drank the hot water, blowing on it as if it were soup. As soon as she finished I put her to bed. Like every evening once she was under the covers she looked around for her teddy bear and hugged it tightly to her chest.

As I was going out of the room she asked if I could lock the door. Silly thing, I said, the only door we lock is the front one! So of course I left the door open with the light from the landing shining onto the bed. I wasn't surprised. At this age night-time fears are common. That's why it's so important to be reassuring, to offer light where there is fear of darkness. And in fact my little ploy worked straight away. Dorrie fell asleep almost immediately, without any more questions.

In the sitting-room I carried on with my knitting until almost midnight. I'm making her a cardigan, with buttons down the front. It's bottle-green, her favourite colour. On the left-hand side I'll embroider some little houses with the sun and a rainbow shining over them.

Dear diary, I went back to the publisher's today. At nine o'clock we had a meeting about that wretched series. Laurie is really pushing to have her own way but I won't give in. Yesterday before going to bed I went to check on Dorrie. She was sleeping like a tired, happy puppy, hanging on tightly to her teddy bear. I had that image in my mind as I explained to Laurie that as she didn't have any children herself, there were some things she simply couldn't understand. You can't go upsetting them with stories of monsters. At the time she took this with a non-committal smile and said nothing. Then later on, at the end of the meeting, she came up to me and asked what I'd done to my eye.

I told her the truth, that I fell down the stairs. She shrugged her shoulders in surprise and said, 'It's not exactly the first time, is it? You don't think you've got a problem with your inner ear?'

She was determined to give me the address of a specialist who has already treated a friend of hers. In the end I took the card with the telephone number and without looking at it I put it into my bag along with all the other papers.

5

I left the publisher's after lunch, at three o'clock. Dorrie's new teacher had called me in for a chat. I wasn't particularly worried. I already knew what she wanted to talk to me about. The child is thin, she doesn't pay attention, she looks a bit run down. I've been told all this before. I told this teacher the same as I've already said to the others: nobody knows how she came into the world, she spent her first few hours in a rubbish bin, in appalling conditions. It's only to be expected that she's not like all the other children. We parted on excellent terms. As I was leaving she asked me if by any chance I'd had a bump in the car. I told her that if you've got low blood pressure it's difficult to see the shelves in the kitchen, even if they've always been in exactly the same place. We laughed. She gets dizzy attacks from blood pressure, too.

On the way back from the school Dorrie, her hand in mine, walked along with her eyes fixed on the ground. 'Good girl,' I said to her, 'when I was your age I used to do that too, there's nothing nicer than looking at the yellow leaves on the ground.'

Jeff was already home. He was lying on the bed with his shoes and jacket still on. The blinds were lowered, the lights out. I realized straight away he had one of his headaches from the tremendous amount of work he does. So as not to disturb him I didn't switch on the lights, I put Dorrie straight to bed and joined him in the bedroom. It does you good now and again to sleep in the afternoon instead of in the evening.

In the middle of the night we got a surprise. Dorrie, in her pyjamas and with her teddy bear in her hand,

6

appeared at the door. First of all quietly, in a low voice, then louder and louder she said she was starving. We ignored her for a bit: it doesn't do to pander to their every whim and fancy! Then since she was still going on, Jeff told her to stop making such a fuss and go back to bed – there were lots of children in the world who were hungrier than her! But Dorrie didn't budge. When she gets something into her head she's harder than stone. Then all of a sudden Jeff pushed back the bedclothes, got up, went over to her, took hold of her arm and took her first into the kitchen and then back into her bedroom. Jeff's a real wonder, even when he's exhausted he can always find a last bit of energy to satisfy the desires of the ones he loves. He must have been away quite a while because when he came back I'd gone to sleep. I turned over and kissed him. I had a hard time getting back to sleep after that though. From the far side of the court-yard came the sound of a cat crying like a child.

Friday, dear diary! Another week over! In just a few days autumn has turned into winter. If you go out now without hat and gloves on you risk getting pneumonia. This morning Dorrie woke up in a right mood. She didn't want to get up, she didn't want breakfast, she didn't want to put her scarf and gloves on. Once we were in the street she didn't want to walk, she said one of her legs hurt. Obviously she was trying it on to get out of going to school. So, very patiently, I told her the story about 'crying wolf'. You mustn't pretend to have aches and pains you haven't got, otherwise when you do get them nobody will believe you. Think of all the children who haven't had the luck to be born like you, with arms and legs!

My little speech must really have got through to her – she set off for school walking quickly in front of me, her head hanging down. As I kissed her at the school gate I realized from her damp eyes that she had been crying. She's such a sensitive child! It just takes a few words put the right way and she grasps everything.

At the publisher's I took the bull by the horns and made a surprise move: I said I would write the first book of the series myself. Laurie didn't make any real objections and neither did the others on the editorial committee. Obviously they will give the final verdict. This weekend I certainly won't have any time for lazing around. As well as thinking about the fairy-tale, which I want to get done quickly, I have to get on with Dorrie's bottle-green pullover.

Saturday and Sunday went by in a flash, as ever. On Saturday it was sunny, so we all decided to take a trip into the country. The air was cold, biting. Dorrie doesn't like going in the car, she didn't want to. She was whimpering. So when we were half-way there Jeff stopped the car, made her get out and suggested that since she's so fond of dogs she could travel in the boot. He shut her in and we went calmly on our way; now and then as we chatted we could hear a kind of dull barking from the back of the car. She's so clever, that child. She was pretending she really was a dog.

Lunch out in the country. I told Jeff about my idea of

writing a book for the series. He was very enthusiastic. He said that instead of trawling around in my imagination I should write the true story of Dorrie. It's a great idea; hers really is a story with a happy ending, a real fairy story.

On Sunday the weather turned bad again. Jeff went out early in the morning. Nothing gets in the way of his sense of duty. Dorrie was asleep until almost lunch-time, so I had the whole morning to work at my desk. In the afternoon I gave Dorrie a little white notebook and asked her to help me write the fairy story. She didn't say anything but she took a pen and sat herself in a corner. While she sat writing like a serious little puppy I went on with my knitting. In a week the pullover will be ready. Just before dinner there was a little squabble: I wanted her to try the pullover on so I could measure the sleeves and she refused. Not that she made a big scene, no. Just that when I called her to try it on, instead of her own arms she kept on holding out to me the arms she had ripped off her doll. So I said that if she wanted, after finishing her pullover I would make an identical one for her doll. She held out her little hands to me and let me put it on.

Jeff didn't come home to dinner. This evening we had the not-dinner dinner. Boiling water. Dorrie drank it down, saying it tasted slightly of mint. When she was already in bed I remembered I had to sign a note giving her permission to go to dance classes. I folded the note and left it on the bedside table. Tomorrow morning you ask Daddy, I said, and like every evening I kissed her on the forehead.

When Jeff got back I was already in bed. I heard him moving carefully in the dark so as not to wake me up. Without opening my eyes I mumbled that he could put the light on because I was awake. He switched it on, undressed and lay down beside me, stroking my face. I'm still thinking about my story. I still haven't got the tone for the beginning right.

Dear diary, Monday again! According to the psychologists there is a definite Monday syndrome. After the relaxation of the weekend all the senses are sort of dulled and refuse to begin the working week. I'm afraid they're right! This morning, in fact, I went and bashed myself on the shelf next to the fridge, and it would be the corner of the shelf, too. A rather bloody cut across my forehead. I tried to stop the bleeding with some ice before Dorrie woke up. Jeff was already up and in the bathroom. When Dorrie came into the kitchen I reminded her of the note for dance classes. She said 'After breakfast', but even after breakfast she didn't want to go to her father. I had to go with her myself to the bathroom door, rap her little knuckles against the wood. Jeff didn't hear her to start off with – as he shaved he was singing his heart out.

When he finally opened the door he did it with such a jolt that Dorrie almost went tumbling to the ground at his feet. I left them alone and went to get dressed. As I was zipping up my skirt I heard Jeff repeating loudly, 'Have you got a tongue in your head or haven't you?!'

Then Dorrie must have plucked up the courage to ask him to sign the note. Jeff, in fact, began cheerfully humming a waltz tune. As I went past the bathroom I peeped in and saw they were dancing. He had lifted her up with his strong arms, made her twirl in the air, when she fell he picked her up off the floor and tossed her up in the air again. After ten minutes of this game he realized he was later than usual for work. Saying goodbye to me and the little girl he hurried out. I went into the bathroom. Dorrie was still lying in the bath. Over-excited, worn out. From the look in her eyes I realized she wouldn't make it to school. Just for once I gave way. It won't be the end of the world! I won't go to the office today, either. I wouldn't like Laurie to see the cut on my forehead and start on at me again to go and see that ear doctor.

It will be a great chance to finish Dorrie's pullover and begin the one for her doll. I've sewn in the first sleeve and I'm about to begin the second. Dorrie didn't manage to get up, but she still wanted me to put her dance costume on. To get it on her I had to put down my knitting. She was so tired she couldn't move her arms or legs. I must tell Jeff not to get her so excited another time. She's too sensitive a child, the slightest thing gets her all churned up. In fact as soon as I put on her leotard she dirtied herself, wetting herself like when she was tiny. Then she threw up her breakfast all over her lace collar. I got a wet cloth and cleaned her all up, but I'd hardly put it in the basin when a trickle of blood came out of her mouth, so I cleaned that up too. She's always too greedy when she eats, and this is what happens. I wanted to tell her off but when I leant over her I realized she was asleep. Never mind, you have to turn a blind

11

eye now and again. I'll make the most of the time and get on with the fairy story. The beginning is decided: the discovery of the baby in the rubbish. But what about the ending? Perhaps there are some good ideas in Dorrie's notebook. I must find it.

They say that ogres don't exist any more but I know they do. My Daddy is a lawyer during the day and an ogre at night. When I'm asleep and I'm afraid the door will open, I hug Teddy. Teddy is my little teddy bear, we've always been friends. He looks as though he's made of material but if I say the right word and kiss him on the heart he comes alive and is stronger than anything. Every evening Teddy promises that if the ogre comes he will look after me. Every morning I promise him that when we are grown up we will run away together. We will wander round the woods looking for the sweetest blackberries and honey to dip our paws into. We will be happy, then, like in all stories with a happy ending.

Love

It had all happened while she was asleep. A sack had been pulled down over her head, like over a kitten being dragged off to the river. Then the sack with her in it had finished up on a lorry. On the lorry there were other sacks in a heap. They were going on a journey, but where to?

Nobody could say. The smaller children were crying, the bigger ones squabbled noisily. After some hours the lorry stopped. The crickets were singing all around, it was still night-time, they were in the countryside. A man with his face covered over climbed up at the back. He made them lie down on the floor and covered them with a canvas sheet. With a threatening voice he said: 'Don't any of you move, no noise, no coughing or laughing. If someone climbs up and asks questions, don't even breathe.'

Then, over the canvas, he laid bales of hay. Soon after the lorry stopped again. More noises outside. Engines being switched on and off. The squealing of wheels, car horns, loud voices. One man did climb up and in a language nobody understood asked lots of questions, the same ones, over and over again. The driver replied quietly, calmly; in the end they laughed noisily. The other man laughed too as he climbed down out of the lorry, they might have been life-long friends.

They continued their journey, hour after hour.

When they got down it was night again. They found themselves squashed together like sardines, locked in a tiny flat. The smallest ones, awake again, had started to cry once more.

They had stayed in that place around a month. With them was a tall man with a moustache who was known as Dragomir. Sometimes he was nice, other times he wasn't. Then he would shout, the veins standing out in his neck, and punch and kick. That happened most often during their lessons. They learned to open handbags, remove wristwatches. He held the bag or the watch, while all the other children crowded around him. The student whose turn it was had first to move quietly up to him then take the object from him with a deft touch, without being noticed. The little ones, who were the most scared, got it wrong most often. If he felt their fingers before the wallet disappeared he would turn round and yell, grab the student by the neck and beat him till the blood came, still shouting at the other children. After they had picked five pockets perfectly the children could leave the flat. Not on their own two feet, but with an elegant man who drove a large, black shiny car without saying a word. The smartest began to disappear after just a week. The others left one by one over the next three weeks.

She had got into that car, too. With her were Alenka, Miranda and Bogoslav. It was such a long journey, a long, long road which the car sped over rapidly. They stopped in a kind of restaurant. The air was hotter than in the city where the flat was. The man made them get out, he bought them sweets, ice-cream and sandwiches. He bought everything they wanted as if they were his own children. When the waiter was there he stroked their hair.

The new city was even bigger, with houses of all shapes and sizes and few trees. They'd gone round all the camps. She had been the last to leave.

For three months now she'd been working on that bridge inhabited by giants with wings and long hair all in white stone. She went backwards and forwards with a piece of cardboard in her hands and since being there she'd heard any number of mothers say to their children, 'You see? Be careful, otherwise the gypsies will carry you off.'

That really puzzled her. She already was a gypsy, so who had carried her off, so far from home?

Vesna was ten years old and had a hare lip. She was born in a tribe in the south of Yugoslavia. Her mother and father had ten other children. With that mouth she would never marry. Before winter they had handed her over to a dealer in exchange for two heavy blankets against the snow.

Her new family was not very different from the one she had left. There was a mother, a father, lots of little brothers and sisters. Mirko, the father, worked with cars and the mother, whose name was Zveva, went begging in the centre with the littlest ones. But in the evening, round the fire or the television, she wasn't allowed to sit next to any of the others. That's how she understood that she wasn't their real daughter, that they weren't related, not even distantly through the tribe. The only thing that mattered to them was that every evening she went back with her pockets full.

It was always Mirko who met her when she came back. He would meet her by the doorway to the tent, his hand outstretched. If there was enough money he gave her a bowl of soup, otherwise he pushed her around and shouted, 'Bitch, do you think this is a hotel? Do you think this is the Grand Hotel or something?'

Some evenings Mirko stayed out with his friends and came back drunk. The she buried her head in her arms and her teeth chattered so hard she couldn't stop them. Her real father used to do the same thing, too. So she ran off fast, as fast as she could before he got his hands on her. She would run swiftly down to the river, leaping like a young hare. On the river bank, hidden among the bushes, she would wait for dawn.

The river! That's what she missed more than anything. It was lovely down there! In winter there was a thick crust of ice with water running beneath. In spring the ice broke and cracked all over with a loud noise. There were the coots whose eggs you could suck, and the quarrelsome pairs of mallards. There were the juicy berries and in summer the cool water to bathe in and the women from the village who went there to wash the clothes and chattered like a radio, never stopping for even a moment.

Under the bridge where she was now there was a river, too, a big river, slow and a bit yellow, but when she went to look at it, it left her completely cold. When she was sad, though, she would shut her eyes; and then its noise became the noise of all rivers and it was as if warmer blood passed around her heart, wrapping her up, warming her inside. Nearly every day she was sad and so nearly every day she played this game.

That morning just before summer she was playing it, too. The air was already very hot and to protect herself she stood in the shadow of an angel. Nobody went by at that time of day. So, covering her face with her hands, she could think in peace about her river, about all the flowers which grew near the water and all the frogs which hid themselves in it.

She didn't hear the footsteps on the pavement. Only, all of a sudden, that voice saying to her, 'Don't you feel well, little one?'

She didn't uncover her face. Close by there must be a father with his little girl. But then a hand stroked her head lightly and so Vesna looked. In front of her was a man whose hair was grey in places and who had on a full white shirt. The man repeated his questions and she didn't say yes or no, she didn't say she was thinking about the river, but with her arm outstretched she skipped up to him and said in a sing-song voice, 'God bless you sir, God bless you and your family, good luck to you, good luck to you and your family, sir . . .'

The man smiled, he looked at her as men look at each other before a knife fight, straight in the eyes as if to read what lies behind them. Still looking at her he slipped his hand into his pocket and pulled out two or three coins. Instead of dropping them from a height he put them right into the palm of her hand, and in so doing touched her. The bridge was still deserted. The man didn't say anything and set off towards the other side, walking with a step that was just a bit too slow.

The tarmac was hot beneath her feet. Did he want to be called back, perhaps? She could follow him, ask for more money for her sick and dying mother. In the meantime the movement of the sun had shifted the shadow of the angel a little further round.

She had very little money that evening. Mirko beat her and she went to bed with nothing to eat. Curling up on the floor she placed the palm of one hand against her cheek. No, it wasn't just her impression, where the man had touched her hand it really was warmer, even after all those hours it was still warm.

Over the next few days the man didn't come by but she saw him several times. He was standing in an enormous poster near the camp and there was a lot of writing next to him. Unlike in real life he had a big black moustache and a pistol strapped over his white shirt. There was no washing machine or fridge beside him. Rather than an advert selling something, it looked like a film. That's it, he's an actor, with those eyes he couldn't be anything else.

Was that the first time he had crossed over the bridge? Yes, almost certainly, because she'd never noticed him before. Perhaps he was a stranger, like her. He lived in

18

a big hotel with palm trees or spent his time on a white beach surrounded by almost naked dancers.

When he saw her lip, instead of laughing or hurrying away he had touched her.

One afternoon Zveva took the girl with her to the centre. They went past two or three big hotels and she looked inside. She looked inside all the taxis, and all the cars with darkened windows.

Ten days later, the skin of her hand was still warm just as it was when he touched it. Before going to sleep she rested it on her cheek, letting it stay there and pretending it was a small, helpless little thing, a kitten or a rag doll.

On the bridge she didn't shut her eyes any more, the river was different now. Even when she was tired she kept them open, like an owl in the middle of the night.

Towards the end of June the city was struck by a series of cloudbursts; the tourists ran about wrapped in coloured plastic raincoats with their bags on their heads.

The sky was the same as she had seen painted in a church in her village, violet, grey, streaked with yellow flashes of thunder. In that storm the big, strong angels were no use at all.

As the water ran down her neck from her hair she realized that the hand which had been touched was becoming damp and cold, just like the other one. It was hours yet before she was to return to the camp, she had time to try and make it warm again. On the road to the cinema the rain turned into pieces of ice, one of her shoes broke and she slipped both of them into her pocket. It was the right cinema, there he was out in front, big, made of cardboard, a gun in his hand. At the box office she pulled out two fistfuls of change. The seated woman counted the coins one by one, then nodded her head and gave her a blue ticket. There was hardly anyone inside, she sat in the front row, her legs stretched out in front of her. That way the actors were talking just to her. He was a policeman, he was called 'The Avenger'. It wasn't his real name but a name the others had given him because he was good. He fought, ran and handled a gun better than anyone else. When the cars were going flat out and smashing all over the place she felt as if she was going to be sick. The man in the white shirt seemed to be losing but then, in the end, he beat everybody else.

The film had ended and started three times. When Vesna reached the road leading onto the bridge the car which took the children back to the camp had already gone. The rain had stopped but the wind was blowing now. What should she do? She didn't know. Lost in thought, she began to walk up and down the nearby streets.

As she looked in a shop at ladies' stockings she heard a sudden screech, the sound of a car. The door opened and before she knew what was happening a hand pulled her inside. How could they have found her? It was Mirko. He said something through gritted teeth, he hit her on the face, on her rabbit lips. Then she remembered she had teeth, a nose, gums, all there, hard as wood. She tasted something warm in her mouth, then everything went blank.

She was woken up by the noise of a chain, it was hers, her ankle was tied to an iron bar. From a nearby tent came the voices of Zveva, Mirko, their children. They were eating. She lay down in a less uncomfortable position. Did she care? Not at all. What she wanted had happened, after the film. One hand was again warmer than the other. She slept a lot those few days, she even dreamed. On the order of the police chief he turned up at the camp with a machine gun in one hand and a dagger in the other. Nobody escaped him. Even Mirko wept and begged. There was the sound of a shot, then silence. Suddenly a light shone full in her face: it was him, he took her in his arms.

There really was a light, but it was Zveva taking off her chain.

She started working again that same day, on the same bridge. It was summer by now, there were lots of tourists, they stuck close together like sheep in the fields or else they went around on their own like deer. With her pieces of cardboard in her hand she went up to everybody. If they didn't give her any money she tried to take it for herself.

One morning a black man set himself up opposite her; he sold necklaces, plastic elephants. When he had customers he kept her at bay with a look, when they were alone he came over to chat. He talked so fast she didn't understand anything he said. Once he hugged her really hard and she gave him a thump in the stomach. A little thump. Her thumps never came out the way she imagined. This one went 'plop', the black man rubbed his

21

stomach and laughed. She wished it had been a much bigger thump.

Who knows why the tourists went about at night-time too? You couldn't see anything at night, only animals in the wood could do that and yet they went around just the same. They were nearly always young. They went around in big groups, often hanging on to each other. They sang tuneless songs, yelling at the tops of their voices. They looked drunk, sometimes they were. The smell of alcohol wafted behind them on the bridge. She followed them, asked them for money. They pretended they couldn't hear her or else they looked the other way, they tossed coins in her direction as if they were playing heads or tails and laughed when quick as a flash she bent down to pick them off the ground. As long as it was still light people passed by solidly like a river, then they passed by in small groups. There was always a bit of time between one group and the next. During one of these pauses the black man came over to her again, gave her a little ring and said, 'You and me engaged' and straight after that stuck his tongue in her mouth. She clamped her teeth together and the black man's tongue was stuck in the middle. He walloped her for that, her head was reeling.

But he didn't manage to hit her a second time. In silence, as if he was walking slightly above the ground, someone had arrived and stopped the negro, grabbing his arm tightly. His shirt was white and billowing. When he pushed the hair away from his face with his hand her heart skipped a beat then began pounding furiously in her throat, and lower down, in her knees. It was him, in flesh and blood, the Avenger!

As soon as the black man moved off, he had insisted that she shouldn't stay on the bridge on her own. She looked at the sky. Judging from the position of the moon it was still some time before the car was due to arrive. Obediently she followed him in silence to a nearby bar. There were lots of tourists sitting at the tables outside. They sat down in the middle of them, the man asked her what she wanted to eat or drink. She wanted to tell him that even without his moustache she knew who he was, she had seen him in a film killing everybody, he was the Avenger. He ordered her a big ice-cream with cream and biscuits, a yellow liqueur for himself. He asked her lots of questions. Did she have a mummy? A daddy? Where was she born, a long way away? Had she ever been to school? She looked like a little lady, a lovely little lady. How old was she? Did she understand or did she only speak the gypsy language? Or perhaps she didn't have a tongue at all?

As he said this the man tickled her under the chin. In the meantime her ice-cream had appeared. There it was in front of her, melting like snow, and she didn't have the courage to eat it.

'Let's see if you really haven't got one,' said the man and piling cream onto the spoon he began to tease her lips. Just like mummy blackbird used to do with her little chicks in the bushes bear the river. Perhaps she was a little chick? She opened her mouth. The slippery, sweet food went down as easily as anything. They got up when

23

the dish was empty. Without a word she took hold of his wrist and led him back towards the bridge. They waited a bit. The moon was low on the horizon again. She couldn't bring herself to tell him the car had already gone. Luckily he spoke first, he said it was pointless standing there until dawn. They crossed the bridge again.

In his house there was heavy furniture and a great big television. He sat her down on the sofa, switched it on for her and disappeared into another room. Just as a cat on the screen was chasing mice, falling off the top of a high building without hurting himself at all, he came back. He was wearing a sort of light coat with nothing underneath. He said, 'Before we go to sleep we'll have a nice bath', and he picked her up off the sofa. He smelt different from Mirko. Instead of frightening her it made her want to lick him.

He wanted to sit and watch as she got undressed. He sat on the toilet with his hands in his coat pockets.

Vesna had never had a bath ... where would she end up if the plug came out while she was still in it? He helped her. With a soft sponge he scrubbed her back, her stomach, he passed it between her legs. He wet her hair, too, letting it float in the water like seaweed. Then with water running down her whole body she got out and he wrapped her in a towel. He dried her very slowly, his hands pausing every now and then.

In the house there was a room she hadn't seen yet. It was bright with a little bed in the middle and lots of toys all around. The Avenger led her with no clothes on into

24

this room and made her lie down under the covers. Then he picked up a book and began to read her a story. It was about a toy soldier with just one leg who fell in love with a toy ballerina made of paper.

When the man's lips rested on hers she jumped because she was already half asleep. She arched her body. Was this how the story ended?

During the night she had a dream. She was a kitten. Her mother was running her tongue backwards and forwards to clean her and she was shaking all over. She was shaking, not like on the bridge when she was cold but as if the warmth of the river was running right through her.

The next morning the Avenger dropped her off not far from the bridge. Before leaving he slipped two or three thousand lire notes into her pocket. She must have been there at her usual time because the tourists weren't about yet, only people hurrying off to work. The day went by the same as all the others. No, not quite the same. When she spied a white shirt amongst all the other shirts her heart leapt into her throat or sank down to her knees.

She hadn't asked him any questions. Nor had he said I'll come back or wait for me. If it had happened once it could happen again. He smelt the way cake-shops smell early in the morning.

That evening she set off punctually to meet up with the car. On the back seat the children who had been picked up first were already asleep. When he saw her there again the driver made no comment, he drove quickly through the city like every other evening. Could it be that at the camp nobody had noticed she was missing?

That must be it. As she went into the tent Mirko didn't beat her. The little boys grabbed hold of her legs as they yelled.

But that wasn't it. When they were all lying down on their beds of straw Mirko came over to her. He spoke in a low voice like he had never done before. He had his trousers open and a hand inside. He lay down beside her and bit her ear, hurting her.

'Whore,' he said, 'you little whore, if you let others do it to you, I'll do it too.' He climbed on top of her, lifted up her skirt. He couldn't get it in first go, nor the second. So he used force, he spread her legs and went into her as you go in through a door when you have lost the key and you kick it down.

He went in and something broke, something tore, the more he went on the more she felt the fire, it burned her so much, so much, each time she hoped he would go out and each time she was wrong, he would never stop.

Then, when she couldn't hope any more, it was all over and he fell on top of her like a dead man. After a bit he went back to his wife's bed, his trousers still open.

Next morning Vesna was on the bridge again. The pain made her walk with her legs stuck together. Every time she ran towards a client she felt a pain inside. Partly because of that, and partly because she was a bit distracted, she earned less than usual those few days.

But instead of beating her Mirko preferred doing the other thing now. She had learnt to imagine that it was the Avenger in his place: she could smell his perfume, she could envisage his flat, hairy stomach. Sometimes she was too tired to imagine anything; then, her head to one side, she would count the objects scattered on the floor.

Several white shirts had passed by, but not his. Where could he be? Perhaps he was fighting another dangerous mission.

Meantime she had found another name for him. A few days before, near the bridge, they'd put up another poster. It showed a woman standing on tiptoe in bra and knickers. In her hand she held a balloon the shape of a heart. There was something written next to her in letters red as a mouth. She asked a young boy who knew how to read what it said. Love, he told her. Love was the heart, it was that thing inside that she felt for him. Love, love, she repeated to herself for days on end as if it was a song with just one word.

One night this is what happened. Mirko realized that she was there only in body and he flew off the handle. He pushed her round the room, against the table corner, against the gas canister. Then he put it in her mouth, he made that disgusting slime come out. She threw up in front of him. Once she was alone she threw up again. She wanted to cry, she shut her eyes tight, she shut them but it didn't do any good.

Next morning, on the bridge, she decided to do a magic trick she learnt as a child. She said the name Love, and spat in a circle again and again. Magic works when you don't use it too often and when your heart is really in it.

It works, of course it works. Just before lunch-time there he is in his white shirt, walking as if he was going nowhere in particular. He walked past her like that, without looking at her. Perhaps she'd forgotten something when she did the magic? Then she shouted Love. That word was like a dart, a knife: it struck him right in the back, and he turned round, he came back with his hands in his pocket.

At his house in the kitchen he put together a little meal just for the two of them. She hadn't even opened her mouth, he'd been doing all the talking. He told her he was a teacher, he taught technical drawing in a school some way away.

It must be a new film, in one he was a policeman, in another a teacher. He had read so many books, he knew lots of things. But he was still strong, you could see all his muscles taut under his shirt, ready to strike.

He wanted her to sit on his lap to eat. He fed her himself, slowly, like little birds in the nest. Then he insisted on her having a bath, he undressed her like the first time and he got undressed too. He said to her you're beautiful, and his hand stroked her back and rested on her bottom. In the water he asked her to show him what she was like inside, to open her legs. She was afraid: what if by chance he noticed that Mirko had been there too? No, she would never open them.

But when he bent over and kissed her with his whole tongue, as if he was looking for something in her mouth, she didn't think of anything any more and her legs opened by themselves. In the warmth of the water she slipped two fingers inside. Sitting on the toilet he held one hand between his legs too, and with his eyes closed he was moving it backwards and forwards.

When she got out of the bath he made her put on a night-shirt. Even though the sun was still up he took her to bed. It was the same room as the other time with the light-coloured bed and all the toys around. She wanted to ask him to go on with the story of the soldier with one leg. Over the past weeks she'd always wondered how it finished but he said, 'Cuddle this and go to sleep' and he gave her a rag teddy. Then he switched off the light and went out without a sound.

Vesna tried to obey him but she couldn't, she closed her eyes as if she were sleeping but she wasn't sleeping at all, she was still awake when he came back, when he gently lifted up her night-shirt and lay down on top of her. The more he moved, the more he said things. Inside herself she was talking, too, and she said 'Love, love, my love . . .'

She stayed in his house four days. They spent all the time having baths, eating, watching television. Every time she was in bed pretending to sleep, he climbed on top of her and moved backwards and forwards. The second day somebody rang the bell. She was afraid it was Mirko. Perhaps Love knew that, because he didn't open the door. He didn't even ask 'Who is it?' The phone rang a few times and before answering he pushed her into another room, telling her to be quiet and not to move.

Then one morning he got up earlier than usual. He made her put on the clothes she always wore. Walking a few steps ahead of her he took her back to near the bridge. He didn't turn round to say goodbye. He didn't promise to come back. But this time she knew he would come back. She was sure of it. The night before, as he moved heavily against her, he had whispered, 'I want you all to myself, little girl, I want a baby just for us.'

Love. She wanted it too. She wanted a kitten she could always give milk to.

She spent the whole day on the bridge, as if she had never been away. When the moon was high up in the sky she went to meet the car. She was a bit afraid but not that much. Would they beat her because she had been away so long? More than likely she would get a real hiding but then she would tell them what had happened. Soon she would get married, she would have a baby then lots of babies and everything would be all right. They might even have a party.

By now the moon had crossed more than half the sky. The car wasn't there. There weren't any other children waiting for it, either. The moon went down a bit further and she still stood there. The only thing to pass by was a police car, which slowed down. She hid behind a big plane tree, she stared at the bark for a while. There were two ants going round and round, they moved their antennae as if they were silently calling to each other.

Could they have forgotten her perhaps? Perhaps they'd left the city? She'd heard Mirko say lots of times, we'll move to the North where people have more money. Or perhaps something else had happened: after leaving her Love had gone to the camp to ask for her hand.

Mirko had refused and he had killed all of them with a single burst of fire. Now he was back home, he was resting, it was up to her to go back to him.

When the sun came up the other side of the sky from the moon, Vesna headed towards his flat. She arrived at the front entrance as the first buses began to pass by. She lifted up her face, the shutters were open, light came out of one of the windows. She touched the bell as if it were a burning coal, just brushing it with her fingertips. She waited a step away from the door, nothing happened. She pressed it again, harder this time. She held her hand there and counted to three. Her heart had begun racing all over her body, it had even turned into breath, it was in her throat, on her tongue, it raced as if she had been running whereas she was standing still.

She didn't have the courage to ring a third time.

Probably, she thought, Love was sleeping soundly, so soundly that no noise could get through his ears. As she waited she realized she was hungry. She found a baker's and spent all her money on brioches and bread rolls. When she finished eating she decided to wait a bit before going back to the front gate. She was free for a bit, she could go for a walk like everybody else, look in the shop windows as long as she wanted.

It was just as she was looking at all the things on display that the idea came. The idea of taking Love back a present. She decided what it would be as soon as she laid eyes on a little pink bar of soap shaped like a heart, lying half hidden among all the other things. The problem was how to get it. If it had been one of those great big shops where nobody takes any notice of you it would have been easy to take it. Instead it was a tiny little shop where the owner stood behind the counter and if she wanted it she needed to have some money first.

There were lots of people in the streets, now. The buses were passing by, weighed down with all the people inside. She chose one at random. It was so crowded she could barely get on.

Elbows, pockets, behinds, bags, elastic, swollen stomachs. How long would the bus take? She had to move fast, get off in the middle of a crowd of people while they were still in the city centre. Schoolboys, men in jackets. Chinese with plastic bags. At last a large, soft leather bag next to an elegant woman.

As her fingers skimmed over the purse she saw Love standing in front of her and she saw herself giving him the heart.

There was a yell. Somebody grabbed her by the hair, somebody else slapped her across the face a couple of times, somebody at the back shouted to the driver 'Stop!' The woman was saying in a shaken voice, 'If you hadn't spotted her I would never have noticed.' The man said 'When you see one of this lot around you always have to keep your eyes peeled.' As he said this he had his hand round Vesna's throat as if it was an umbrella handle. The police arrived with their sirens blaring, they didn't have to climb on the bus because somebody kicked her off.

The blue and white car drove fast and made a noise as if she was the most important person in the world. They dropped her off in a big building in a room where there were lots of other people. They were all sitting on two benches against the wall, they were looking down at the floor or they held their hands over their face so as not to see anything at all. After a long time they called her. Her feet were cold and her stomach was empty again. What if Love saw she wasn't coming home and that she wasn't on the bridge and thought she had gone away for ever, that she didn't care about him any more?

When the woman in uniform behind the table asked her name, all of a sudden and without knowing why she burst into tears. Behind her a man exclaimed, 'They're all the same, this lot, with their crocodile tears!'

The woman leaned towards her and with a kind voice asked her again, 'What's your name?' The man in the first apartment, the one who had taught her lots of things, had said: 'Never tell them your real name'. When the woman asked the question for the third time Vesna raised her head and with her eyes still damp murmured, 'Love'.

How old was she? She held out two hands with all her fingers sticking up.

Later on she got into a van with some other girls. There were two tiny little windows with a wire mesh over them so you could hear all the noise from outside but you couldn't see anything. They got out in a great big concrete courtyard with two trees in the middle. She had to wait again in another room. Then a woman called her, they photographed her, gave her a number, weighed her, measured how tall she was. Once, with her real father, she had gone to take their only horse to a place almost exactly the same as this one. They'd measured it, weighed it, dragged it into another room. It had come out flat on the floor, the white star in the middle of its forehead had gone red and was gushing like springs in the rock. Was the same thing about to happen to her?

The lady who came to fetch her had a hard job getting her to follow. She was in another room again, there were two chairs, a table, the lady showed her some ink blots one after the other, she asked her what was this, what was that. What else could they be if they weren't blots? They were just blots. Then in a calm voice she had asked her lots of questions. How old was she really? Where were her mummy, her daddy, her little brothers and sisters? Had she been to school? Could she read, write, did she know why she was there? Then the lady got up and said, 'All right then, when you decide to talk you only have to call me.'

She gave her a pen, a sheet of paper. She pointed to where she should sign. Your signature, she said again, your name in other words. If the name was Love, what would the signature be? A heart, that was it. She took the pen as if it was a spoon and slowly, paying careful attention to the outlines, she drew a heart.

Over the next few days nothing happened. She was in a room with other girls. When it was time to eat she ate, when it was time to go out she went out into the court-yard. If it hadn't been for Love, she would have been absolutely fine there: nobody bothered her, she ate several meals a day, she slept as much as she wanted. When she was lying on her camp-bed she told herself the story of the one-legged soldier, just to feel him close.

The story went like this. The soldier arrived in a lovely

34

house in a box together with lots of other soldiers who had both legs. A ballerina lived there too. The ballerina had two legs as well but as she held one in the air she looked like she only had one. So the soldier falls in love. But they are a long way apart and he can't talk to her. One day the soldier is by the window, there's a gust of wind and he falls down. A small boy puts him into a little paper boat, the little paper boat is swept along by the current, it reaches a fish and the fish eats it. So the one-legged soldier finishes up in his tummy as if he was a baby.

That was as much as she knew of the story, but it couldn't end quite like that because she'd seen there were lots of pages still to read so the story went on some more before it came to an end.

One day as she was telling this story to herself a woman came to the door and said Love in a loud voice. When she heard that name she jumped as if she'd stepped on a thorn. She went through the corridors alongside the woman, shuffling a bit.

Love must be there, behind one of those doors. Would he fling his arms round her neck as soon as he saw her? Yes, and with his strong arms he would lift her into the air. Then they would leave this place. A car was waiting outside for them. It would drive off fast with both of them inside.

When the woman rested her fingers on the doorhandle she steadied herself a little, ready for Love's embrace. The door opened . . . It wasn't Love, but a man in a white coat.

The man said, 'Here's love!' He lifted her up, put her

on the narrow bed and said, 'Take your knickers off.' He wasn't like Mirko, nor even like the Avenger. Instead of his thingy he put a metal instrument inside. Instead of saying kind or nasty words he stayed silent. In the end, even though he didn't get his hands dirty, he washed them under the tap. As he washed them he went mmmmm, and when she had her knickers back on and got down from the bed, he said to her 'Did you know? There's a little baby in there.'

Had he put it in there, stuck it in with that shiny cold instrument? That couldn't be right, she'd had a good look at it before he'd put it in, it looked like a spoon, a bit like a funnel and a bit like a spoon and there was nothing on top of it or inside it. So it was Love, then, Love who had put it in her that last night without her noticing. He had said I want all of you, I want a baby for us, and there the baby was. It had settled in there like in a little house.

That was why over the last few days she hadn't been at all hungry. She could eat as much as she wanted but she didn't want anything, only to throw up. Yes, to throw up like that time Mirko put it in her mouth. And he was growing inside there, he'd already been growing day after day. Sometimes you break open eggs to eat them but you can't eat them because instead of yolk there's a kind of spittle. A spittle that's a bit harder than spittle.

Once she'd had a close look at it, on the spittle there was what looked like two eyes, a soft and half-open bit that looked like a beak. If it could stay in there a bit longer it would almost certainly become a chicken.

In place of her stomach now she had an egg and this

36

egg would grow more and more until you could see there was something inside. It was growing, growing. In February if you lift up the clods of heavy earth you can see underneath grass which is already thick grass but which is under the ground.

It was growing, she thought, and with her hands over her stomach she lay down on her camp-bed.

The next morning she wasn't there any longer but sitting in a train with a lady who held her by the hand. They had told her she was too little to stay there and they had taken her to the station. She had never been on a train. It was lovely. If you sat on one side the world went forwards, if you sat on the other side it went backwards. What made it even nicer was that all that movement was taking her back to Love. Nobody had actually said that, but she knew anyway. There are some things you just know, like birds know when winter is coming. The lady was kind, now and again she asked, 'Do you want something to eat? Do you want to go to the toilet?'

But she didn't want anything, she only wanted to get there soon, as soon as she could.

Then she fell asleep. As her head rolled from side to side she had a dream. Instead of her own face she had the face of the angel on the bridge. Her face was made of stone, it was crumbling away all over and there was nothing she could do. When she tried to make it stop she heard the voice of her real mother. She shouted her name across the fields round about, but couldn't make her answer. She sat in a bush and she had an egg between her legs. The egg opened and instead of a chicken an angel came out, an angel like the one on the bridge but light as air, so light that he took her by the hand and carried her with him into heaven. She didn't find out what heaven looked like because suddenly she was in Love's house. She was alone in the flat and she knew he was coming. She was so happy she moved backwards and forwards like dogs do when they are happy. She heard footsteps on the stairs. She was there when the door opened and instead of Love it was her father. He grabbed her by the arm, twisted it behind her back and she fell to the ground. As she fell she hit her head hard on the floor.

Suddenly she woke up. Where was she? Oh yes, she was on the train.

Outside the world wasn't going anywhere any more. It was dark and you couldn't see anything. But now, all of a sudden, she knew where she was going. She was going back to her real parents and her real brothers and sisters, there by the river.

She shook the lady by an arm, shouted 'Pee-pee'. She stayed in the toilet for a while. The lady stood outside and knocked on the door now and again. When the train slowed down she drew her stomach in as far as possible, she tried to become like one of those flat, slippery creatures who live in the water and suck blood. In this fashion she wormed her way out of the window and as soon as the train slowed down a bit more she let herself fall. There was grass below, as it was autumn it had stopped growing.

It took her four full days to get back to the city where

Love lived. She got in and out of cars and lorries. Some drivers asked something in return for taking her and she gave it to them as she had to Mirko, without thinking about anything. When she reached the outskirts of the city it was already pitch black. Instead of going straight to his house she slipped inside the front entrance to a block of flats. She hid between the stairs and the cellars. She didn't sleep at all. It was the last, absolutely the last night not in a bed. Could angels' wings move down invisibly to your feet, taking the place of your shoes? That's what would happen to her next morning, she would fly towards him. Instead of going up the stairs she would fly straight to the window of Love's house. At that time he was still asleep, asleep like a child. She would watch him sleeping for a bit then she would tap her knuckles gently on the window. Then he would jump up and open it. She would hop inside and show him her stomach, the egg that was growing in her stomach. And after that they would live happily ever after.

When dawn came she reached the city centre by bus. From there she went on by foot. She still had her old shoes on, no wings had sprouted in their place. Instead of flying she had to look up at his window. Two windows were lit and one open. When she rang the bell the sound went up a secret passageway to the flat and came down again through the open window. Her heart had landed down by her knees and she didn't know how to get it to come back up again. She rang again, her heart throbbed in her throat and nothing happened. Or rather something did happen, but she didn't know if it was real or not.

Behind the curtain a figure appeared rapidly. It looked like the figure of a woman.

What if Love had gone to live somewhere else while she was away, in a bigger house? There was only one way she could find out, by asking other people who lived in the block. Two people came out of the front entrance. When a third one came out, a rather chubby child, she slipped in through the open door behind him. She ran up the stairs two by two and stood outside the door for a moment to catch her breath. On the landing she noticed something she had never noticed before. Even if she stood absolutely still she wasn't really still, there was something moving in her stomach. Was that him already? Did he want to come out so soon? If he saw him already out, Love might think he belonged to someone else. He had to wait a bit longer. She put a hand on her stomach and told him in a low voice, 'There's no hurry. Soon we'll spend all our time together, you, me and Daddy too.'

Then she stood on tiptoe and rang the bell. The sound of the bell was much louder there, you could hear everything behind the door. In fact she did hear, she heard a little boy's voice saying 'Who on earth could it be at this time in the morning?' and a woman's voice reply 'Maybe it's a telegram' and the sound of her steps as she came towards the door. Her hair was hanging over her face and she pushed it back over her shoulder and stood up straight. But the woman never appeared before her. From the other end of the flat a man's voice called out. 'Don't open the door!' the voice shouted. 'At this time of day it can only be gypsies or Jehovah's Witnesses!'

Love.

For a moment she thought, 'It isn't true. It sounds like him but it isn't.' Even if she'd wanted to leave she couldn't. Her feet had turned to wood. The wood with all its roots was spreading up her legs and over her whole body. Her heart was still there, but it was stone now, a stone which had stopped beating. As she stood there she heard his voice again.

'Finish the story,' said the child's voice and the man's voice said, 'You're already late, I'll finish it this evening before you go to bed.' It was the same voice as in the film, exactly the same. Love's voice.

Even if stones fly up in the air a little way they fall down again. She went down the stairs without seeing anything. She went down below the ground floor, down to the basement. If there hadn't been a wall there she would have gone further. When she reached the wall her ankles then her knees crumpled and she sat down heavily.

She wasn't hungry or sleepy and she didn't want anything. She barely knew where she was. Something was moving in her stomach. Was it the almost spittle? Yes, it must be him. He wanted to come out, to see the light. But it was dark there and you could hardly see anything and there was a bad smell too. If she told him a story would he promise to stay still and not give her any more trouble? She only knew one story, the same one: about the two who fall in love because they both have only one leg. He was a soldier, she danced. He was much more in love with her, in fact she didn't love him at all because he was a long way away and she couldn't see him. Then

41

one day a terrible thing happens. He falls out of the window and a fish eats him. Everything is dark inside the fish and he doesn't know what is happening. So he thinks, once before when I was spittle I was inside a stomach. One day the fish is caught and a man eats it all up, nobody knows what happens to the soldier, but nobody loved him so it doesn't matter very much. Meantime the ballerina has fallen in love with another soldier. He has three legs and they get married and live happily ever after because he gives her one of his legs.

She wondered what stories babies liked listening to before they were born. Hers didn't like that one at all. He didn't like it so much that he came out into the darkness, she could feel him dribbling down her legs in the middle of something warm which must be blood.

A Childhood

First Conversation

Imagine this, for example. Two cars set off at the same time from opposite directions. One of them should have left earlier but at the last minute the owner gets a telephone call that lasts half an hour. If he hadn't gone to answer the phone would he have left at the right time? But no, he does go to answer it and he's late. So both cars leave at exactly the same moment. Then a large lorry overturns on the same road they are both travelling along. It is quickly towed away, but there's still a patch of oil on the road. At exactly that point one of the two cars is travelling very fast. Which lane is the oil on? His. The other one is driving slowly, he's thinking about his wife who's been poorly for some time and whom he wants to take to a doctor. In a flash he realizes that a car in the other lane is heading straight for him. The car crashes into him. He doesn't have time to think anything else because he dies on the spot. If he'd let the phone ring instead of answering nothing would have happened.

Someone else would have died in his place, or maybe nobody would. Maybe the person who should have died is at home in his slippers in front of the television, he's sitting there and he sees that terrifying accident. Isn't that the road he came by? Yes, that's the one. At the same time even. What a piece of luck says his wife, running her fingers through his hair. Luck. You see? Luck. Anyway, let's go on. There are children who when they are six years old say I want to be a doctor, and then they are. Others want to be engineers, missionaries, mechanics, and they are. At school I had a friend who by the age of five could already take apart all the electrical gadgets in the house and put them back together perfectly. He wanted to be a physicist, it was in his blood, do you see? In his blood or somewhere else anyway somewhere or other it was written Giovanni will do this and Giovanni does it because he can't do otherwise. The same with me. A lucky child. The day I learned to ask questions I knew what was in store for me. I wasn't born to cure people or build machines, I was born to bring order to the things around me. I came into the world in autumn, you know the day and the month, you've read them in the file. I mention it because that comes into it too. My sign's horoscope underlines a meticulous and stubborn patience, a marked tendency to order. It's in the spirit of the season: everything is dying, it sinks down below, mixes together and goes rotten in order to be reborn again. Introspection, analysis, rigour and prodigious memory are characteristics of people born in this period. The same with me. I don't remember but I think that more or less straight away from when I first learned to use my tongue I began to ask questions. I went out with my mother and I would ask her what's this, what's that? And she would answer that's a stone, that's a bird.

It was and it wasn't. Because the stone was a bit different every time and the bird was small and brown or big and black with a yellow beak. I had to bring order into the world; to do that I had to know names. So I asked again, what's this, what's that? But she would answer stop being silly, I've already told you and she pulled me along by the arm. My mother was already working as a nurse then. When I went with her to the hospital her colleagues would pinch my cheeks. They said to me, aren't you happy? You have the best mummy in the world! She was good, in fact, it was just that she had no patience. At the dinner table that's all I thought about, about names, and I would eat my food slowly. She was always in a hurry though. So to get the food down me she would hold my nose. When I couldn't breathe any more I would open my mouth and she would promptly stick the fork down my throat. We had a lot of fights over meat. I didn't like it, I still don't like it.

I've always had a horror of blood.

Second Conversation

She started that job soon after I was born. But it was much more than just a job to her. At Christmas she always got dozens and dozens of Christmas cards. She put her heart and soul into her patients. But at home she was always tired, so I soon learned it was better not to bother her with my questions. I asked them and answered them myself. Then luckily I started school. At school I learned to read. That's when my sense of order really began to take shape. I sat with my books on my knees, reading aloud for hours. I read slowly, spelling out one word after another. There was a drawing and a name next to it. That's how I learned that the bird with the red breast was a robin, that the almost transparent stone was quartz. Each new discovery was a thrill. Something took the place of all the disorder around me. If I didn't do it nobody else would. I had to do it.

Stones were my first passion. They were the easiest thing to catalogue. They don't move, you only have to bend down and pick them up. By the time I was seven I already had more than a hundred of them. I hadn't told my mother, no. Partly because I was a bit scared, partly because I wanted to give her a surprise. One day I would be a famous scientist, a really famous scientist. She would read about me in the papers. One day she would open the newspaper and she would see a photograph of her son. At first she might think it was a mistake. But then, as she read the article, she would realize it was true, that her son was one of the most famous scientists in the world. Then she would forgive me everything. She would hug me like she hugged her patients when they got better.

At that time we often slept in the same bed. She didn't invite me in, it was me who crept in when she was asleep. The sheets were cold and she lay with her body all huddled up on one side. She looked like a mountain climber on the edge of a gulley. I liked pretending to fall too, so I would hold on tight behind her, and together we would fall until almost morning. I went back to my own bed just before the sun came up.

One thing made her angry, yes, the fact that I would never look her in the face. In fact I always had my eyes on the ground. The stone habit, I think. I don't know, I never looked my teacher in the face either, not her, not the teacher, nor anybody else. She would say look at me! and I would go red. Then she would say look at me! again and my neck would bend over at right angles to my body. Then she would take hold of my chin and pull it up, she pulled and tugged until it went crack and I closed my eyes. I closed them and she would prise them open with her fingers, she pushed up my eyelids as if they were two curtains. She would stare into my eyes and yell Look at me! Look at me! She used to say that people who won't look you in the face are either cowards or have something nasty to hide. I couldn't tell her about the stones, it was supposed to be a surprise for when I was grown up. So I was always getting belted.

At the same time as the uncles started coming I got into the habit, just before going to sleep, of repeating the names of all my stones. Not looking at the stones, but with my eyes closed beneath the covers. I was sure that if I repeated them all correctly nothing bad would happen.

The uncles were friends of my mother's. They came after dinner. There were lots of them, all different, and none of them spoke much to me. They used to hurt her,

47

I'm sure of that. Lots of times I heard her moans even with all the doors closed. That's why I daren't make a mistake when I was repeating the names of the stones, because otherwise she would die. No, she doesn't have the faintest idea that if she's still alive it's thanks to me. Order, introspection, prodigious memory, you see? Even then I had to the utmost degree all the gifts of a great scientist.

Third Conversation

At school I was hopeless. I didn't like the other children. They were noisy, they yelled at the top of their voices for no reason. Now I think I would have liked to be like them: to shout, get myself dirty, be naughty and get punished. But at the time I was wrapped up in other things. The teacher would explain fractions and I would think how is it possible that there are so many shapes in the world? Why not one bird but so many different ones? Why not stop at the mouse, why have squirrels and beavers too? Of course I knew nothing about evolution, the whole history of advantageous mutations, of eating and being eaten, of finding your niche and staying tucked away and secure until a new order arrives. Fifteen years ago they didn't tell children these things.

Nowadays they know everything by the time they're six. They know about dinosaurs and why they disappeared. They know how babies come into the world and how the galaxy will end. But not in my day, no, we knew nothing. At most the teacher would say 'One day God woke up bored and so, to pass the time, he made the world, he took six days to do it, one day for each thing, and on the seventh which was a Sunday, he rested.' I believed all this and didn't believe it at the same time. When I thought about God's forehead beaded with sweat and his enormous muscled, tired arms, his fingers trembling slightly, I didn't believe it any more. Before lessons we would always recite a prayer, we said, Almighty God who art in heaven . . . Well, if he was almighty, how come he got tired? I just couldn't swallow the whole thing, right? So I carried on thinking about things, and names, and I was hopeless at school. Once a year the teacher called my mother in and said the child is apathetic, slow, he doesn't take any interest. At home she didn't tell me off, no. She said, why don't you go out into the courtyard and play with the other children? and she would push me outside. Sometimes she would look at me without saying anything and just sigh. She would sigh like dogs do when they're about to go to sleep. But then she had her work at the hospital, the uncles who came to see her, and she often forgot about me altogether. She would say: if you carry on this way you'll end up as a shop assistant and I would just nod. I said yes, all right, I'll sell material or sausages even though I was sure I would be a famous scientist.

If truth be told I could always answer the teacher's questions. She would ask who knows why this is such and such? And even before she had finished speaking I already knew. I knew inside but I kept quiet. I thought that can't be the answer, there must be a catch, it's too easy, there's nothing easy in the world and so I kept quiet. Then someone else answered and it was exactly what I had thought and I sat up straight at my desk and looked around in amazement, was it really so simple? And before a minute had passed I knew that that was only one possible answer, that there were over a thousand right answers. Everything was like that, a bit true and a bit not. What was important was to know that and, knowing it, to make some sort of order.

Naturally I preferred mathematics to all the other subjects. I wasn't very good at that either but I liked it anyway. If a bath tap pours out four litres a minute and the bath holds sixty, how long will it take to fill it to the top? All the baths were filled up in the right amount of time except mine. My bath had a bit of ceiling fall into it, along with the lady from upstairs, so instead of just coming out of the tap the water overflowed and as well as the spilt water there was also a dead body, the lady from upstairs.

You see? I had a real talent. If someone had realized that then perhaps everything would have gone differently. You remember the cars from the other day? That's the way things are. A question of movements which happen at the right time or don't.

Fourth Conversation

I would like to go on talking about school. At home I was almost always on my own. I would think and I always

50

thought I was right, while in class other people had other ideas and so differences of opinion would emerge.

Certainly teachers should be educated a bit better. Apart from history and geography they should teach them some delicacy. I don't know if it's something you can teach or if it's something you already have inside, but my teacher certainly didn't have any. She was always shouting and if she wasn't shouting it was because she was tired.

One day in our Italian lesson she gave us an exercise to do. A composition entitled 'My Daddy'. How old was I? About eight, eight at the most.

Anyway I'd never met my daddy face to face, so as soon as I heard the title I went up to her desk and said quietly, excuse me miss I can't do it. She leaps up and shouts, you'll do it, you'll do it the same as everybody else! Now the problem was this, I had never laid eyes on him, but I knew what he did and I also knew not to say what he did because it was a secret. Secret, exactly. He was a secret agent. To tell the truth nobody had ever told me that. It was me who had guessed. I'd guessed and then I'd asked my mother and she hadn't said yes and she hadn't said no. That's how I realized it was true, that he was a secret agent. That's why he was never home.

So I get a piece of paper and I write, 'I don't know my father because he does a job that nobody is allowed to know about. I know that he's tall, strong, and a good shot with a gun. He's got big strong hands and he always keeps his nails short. He's a karate champion and can kill a bull with a single blow. I never know where he is or what he is doing but I can say that his job is to protect the good countries from the bad ones. One day when his mission is finished he will come and collect me from school. Perhaps he will come with his gala uniform and red sash and all the rest. Then everybody will see who my father is, but in the meantime nobody is supposed to know about it because he is a secret agent and he risks his life every day.' Underneath I had written, 'This essay should be destroyed once it has been read.'

I put in that last line because I trusted the teacher, otherwise I wouldn't have written any of it. But what does she go and do the next day? She comes into the classroom with all the exercises in her hand, she sits down and says 'fibbers will always be found out' and she starts reading my essay out loud. I don't know where to look and all the others are laughing. Then she gives it back to me and says loudly, you would do better to study rather than make up fibs. Everybody starts pulling my leg after that. When we go out of school they push and shove each other and shout 'Is that your father?! Or that one over there?! Oh no, there he is over there by the tree! He's an agent so secret that you can't even see him!'

Everyone else's mother or father always came to pick them up from school. I never understood why. It's ridiculous if you think of the short distance between school and home. Don't you think many parents are over-cautious? Anyway nobody ever came to collect me. My mother couldn't because she was working. I always waited for my father but he never came anyway.

The following year my classmates were still taking the mickey out of me. Children are rather stupid, aren't they? When they find something funny they do it over and over again. In the meantime though, something had happened over the summer. I had grown a lot, I had developed into a strong boy, stronger than all my classmates. So, I put up with it all a bit longer. Then one day it happens. Nobody comes to collect the top boy in the class. He's a fragile child, with blond, fine hair like a girl's. Usually his mother is there every day, waiting for him just outside the gate in her fur coat, smiling. He doesn't know what to do, so I say don't worry I'll take you. I take his arm as if I was much bigger than him. I had a bit of a job persuading him to go into the park. It was almost dusk, he didn't want to. Before opening my trousers I made sure there was nobody around, then I clamped my hand on his neck like a vice and I made him suck until he couldn't breathe for the tears. 'What does your father do?!' I shouted at him all the time. 'What does he do, then?!' He got away from me and ran off, I yelled after him, 'If you tell anyone I'll smash your face in.'

But he did tell, he told as soon as he got home. His parents phoned my mother. She answered the phone, she threw the receiver down. She beat me with her shoes, with the broom handle. She went crazy. She was foaming at me, 'You're like your father, you son of a bitch, that's what you are, a son of a bitch.'

I found out about their affair later on. Yes, she told me about it in another moment of anger, shouting. That day my father was drunk, she was a bit tipsy. There was an end-of-course party for the nurses. He was a consultant, already married and with two small children.

My mother wanted to and didn't want to at the same time. You know how these things are when you've had too much to drink? You do things without thinking straight. Then when it happened she thought about it too much. It wasn't so easy then. My mother was very young, she had no money, she didn't know who to turn to. One day she said yes, the next she said no, she hoped he would acknowledge me, that he would give her some money.

By the time he told her that if she'd gone with him so easily she was sure to have gone just as easily with everybody else and so that baby had absolutely nothing to do with him, it was too late. I was already growing inside, it was too late to turn me out now.

Fifth Conversation

After that business in the park relations between us were rather cooler. When she was home she moved about the rooms as if I wasn't there. I was there but she pretended I wasn't. If she cooked lunch or dinner she left it for me there on the table. I almost always ate on my own. Occasionally she still got angry. She got angry not so much with me as for reasons of her own. Then she would shout, 'I'll get rid of you! I'll shut you up in school! They'll make you pull your socks up' and she carried on shouting for a bit. I ignored it though. I knew she didn't have any patience, that she got things out of her system like that and then she calmed down again.

By now I had over three hundred minerals, a proper collection. That was the time when I got a geology textbook from the school library. It had everything in it: when the earth was born, when stones were crushed together and even why they were still attached to each other. With the help of that book I had begun to write a long detailed entry on each mineral. I had lots of pieces of paper of different colours. On one I would note, this is pirite, you find it in such and such a place. Inside it's like this, even if you can't see it. It's used for this and this. It came into my possession this day of that month and so on.

In this way time went by quickly and I didn't even notice what was happening around me. I hadn't paid any particular attention to one uncle who was coming to the house much more often than the others and I hadn't even realized that my mother shouted much less than usual.

Then one Sunday morning what happens is this, the uncle comes to the house in his sports car, picks me up and takes me off with him. Along the way he tells me he is a doctor, that he met my mother between ward rounds. So far so good, I think. No, all this was before I knew my father was a doctor too. So, chatting about this and that we get to a beach. It was winter, I remember that clearly. There was nobody there, amongst the stones you could see tin cans, some plastic bottles. I was a bit uneasy, that's true. Anyway, we are almost at the water's edge and there he bends down, picks up a stone and throws it into the water. The stone leaps up from the surface three times like a live thing, the fourth time it sinks under the water. I look at him and I don't say anything. But he picks up another stone and puts it in my hand and says here, you try. I don't want to try. I hold it in my hand, I turn it over and over and don't do anything. Then he starts taunting me. He says, 'You don't want to throw it because you can't. You're afraid of losing, of looking silly.' I listen to him for a bit perfectly calmly but then I get fed up. Of course I know how to throw stones and I lift my arm... and just as I'm standing there ready and concentrated, ready to throw, what happens? He brushes his hand over my hair and says, 'I love your mother and she loves me too. Soon we'll get married and all three of us will go and live together.'

That's what he says and I throw the stone just the same, but I'm not concentrating now and as soon as it hits the water it sinks, it goes straight down like lead.

Then we go and have lunch together at home. Mum had cooked chicken and potatoes, he had brought a sweet. Everything's fine up to the cake, the two of them are laughing and joking, I sit in silence. Then, when Mum puts my slice on the plate, I don't know why but I shout 'I'm not eating it!' She starts going on at me 'but you've always liked sweets' and so on and I shout again 'I won't eat it, it makes me sick!' Finally I get a slap. She hauls me into the other room and there she hisses in my ear so that he can't hear:

'I won't let you spoil this one too, do you understand? I won't let you. I'll kill you with my own hands first.'

That same night I wake up with a start. I sit bolt upright in bed and suddenly I do something I had never done. Incredible, isn't it? I start to cry.

Two days later I've still eaten nothing. I'm still sitting there on the bed crying. Then Mum comes up to me sweet as pie, she runs her hand through my hair. As she does that she asks, 'What are all these tears for? because of what I said the other day? Come off it, you're big enough to understand that I was only a bit edgy, why are you still crying?'

I say, 'I don't know, it's not because of that, I don't know why I'm crying' and I hide my face in the pillow. Then she says, 'All right, when you've had enough your dinner's waiting for you.'

To tell the truth I knew perfectly well why I was crying but I couldn't tell her.

Beneath its hard crust the earth has a heart of molten fire. It's all closed in down there, compressed, but if something is broken, in an earthquake for example, this molten heart comes up and up until it comes out of the taps and one day it comes out instead of the water and kills everybody. It would kill Mum, too, she always opens the washing machine without looking inside first.

That's why I was crying, just for that.

Sixth Conversation

For a long time there was no more talk about that business, about any marriage. Sometimes the uncle stayed the night or else he came to fetch my mother and they went to the cinema or to dinner with one of his friends. I neither liked him nor disliked him. Nothing. He just seemed to me like a piece of the furniture, he was there and I tried to keep out of his way. I think he thought of me in the same way, a bedside table, a sideboard or something of the kind. Mum was the bed and I was the bedside table. He had no choice but to keep me too.

Anyway, after a few months the summer comes. School finishes and Mum says I look peaky and she sends me into the country for a while with one of her sisters. It was nice there. I wandered around the fields all day and nobody bothered me. I was still collecting stones. Spending all day long from morning to evening in the open air I began to get interested in birds too.

I had a little white notebook. I always carried it with me and every time I saw an animal whose name I didn't know I wrote down in my notebook where I had come across it and what it was like. When I got back to the city I was on cloud nine. As well as knowing three hundred stones, now I knew a couple of dozen birds as well. A whole new field of study was opening up before me in which I could excel.

Mum came to meet me at the station. There was a brand new car waiting for us over the road. We get in and while she's driving through the narrow streets I make to get out my white notebook. I've got it in my hand when I notice she's going the wrong way. So I tell her. I say, 'Hey, where are we going?' and without looking me straight in the face she changes gear and says, 'Your uncle and I got married, we'll all be living together in his house.'

So the notebook slips back into my pocket and I look

out of the window. I think, what's going to happen when my father comes back?

That's what's in my mind, because I've never seen a triple bed, not even in the biggest shops. Meantime we reach the new house. It's a detached villa with a garden and a big gate. The gate opens without touching it and we go inside.

The house is on two floors with a big white staircase joining them. He's standing at the top of the stairs, his arms folded over his chest, and he watches us coming up. I can clearly remember seeing his smile, I was watching it as I walked up step by step and the more I saw of it the less I liked it. Well, finally we're on the same level as him and to my surprise he takes me in his arms. There I am, not knowing where to look or to put my hands, and he says 'Do you like the new house?' And then, 'If you want now you can call me Daddy.' I answer no under my breath, so quietly that nobody hears or they pretend not to hear.

It's almost lunch-time. My mother takes me to my new room. It's so big I think, why aren't there skates to go with it? But there I am and I start putting my clothes in the cupboard. Over lunch they are grinning like in the films and after a bit they say, 'We've decided to give you a present for our wedding. What would you like most in the world? A bicycle? A leather football?' I think and think and then I say, 'I want a big cage and a pair of birds.'

'Oh no! They're dirty, they make a noise! You've no need for them,' says Mum, but he says, 'No, Rita. Promises are promises! He wants some birds? We'll get them for him.'

So that afternoon we all go off out together, we go to a special shop for birds. I'm quite pleased. I go with the idea of two ravens but we agree on two olive-coloured budgerigars. The man who sold them to me said they were husband and wife so I spent all my time in front of their cage. There I was, waiting, I wanted to see if they loved each other.

I told you, didn't I? Up to now I'd only thought about stones, I knew next to nothing about these things. If I hadn't bought those two birds perhaps nothing would have happened. Who knows? It's always the same question, the question of the two cars.

In any case, they gave them to me and I start watching them. I spend hours by the cage and I write: at eleven thirty he hops up onto the right-hand perch, she looks up at him and stays still. At eleven thirty-three she flutters over to the left and so on and so forth.

I'd seen the films on television. People who love each other kiss, I was sure of that. But not them, they jumped up, they jumped down, they ate, drank, dirtied the cage with that yellow shit of theirs, they went cheep cheep and that was it.

Then one day while we were having dinner it happens. I hear a strange sound from the cage which was in the kitchen so I shift my chair and get up. I go to see if that noise was love or not. It was, they were standing really close and rubbing their beaks like swords. So I calmly go back to the table, I sit down and pick up my fork but before the lasagne reaches my mouth Mum says, 'Who told you you could get down from the table?!' I look at her and look at her but I don't understand. Perhaps you need a licence to get down from a chair like you do to drive a car?

So I don't say anything and carry on eating.

But she won't let it go. She says, 'Apologize to your father.'

'Apologize', I answer, 'to who?'

'You know perfectly well who your father is,' she says and she is already a bit green under the eyes.

'I know and I don't know,' I answer.

'You know perfectly well,' she says and tilts her chin towards her husband.

So I say quietly, 'It's not true,' and carry on eating.

Then his voice chimes in, 'You live in my house and you eat my food. I'm your father now. Apologize.'

You see how difficult it was to work out what was going on. Well, to cut a long story short, we go on a bit like this and the longer it goes on the more confused it gets. Both of them would say something and I wouldn't know what to answer. Then all of a sudden he gets up and says, 'The trouble with this boy is he's never had a firm hand' and before I realize what's happening I'm down from my chair too. He grabs my arm and twists it until the pain makes me fall to the floor. Then he looks down at me and says again, 'Are you going to apologize?' I look at his shoes, I can hardly breathe now for the pain so I open my mouth and a word comes out, that word, sorry.

When I'm back on my chair again and he's sitting on his, he smiles, pleased with himself. He says, 'We're turning over a new leaf today!' He says that and as he says it I'm sure it's not me but somebody else who said that word.

Until that moment I had never noticed that instead of one there were two of us.

Seventh Conversation

The days went like this: I went to school and they went to work together. I would come home while they were still at the hospital and I was on my own until dinner time. The arrangement was that in the afternoon I would study. I was at secondary school now and I had piles of homework, but studying was the last thing I wanted to do. I had so many ideas in my head, so I would go out and wander around till evening. Sure, there were particular places I headed for, I went some ways more than others. More than anything I liked the road down to the sea.

It wasn't unusual to see big and small grebes flying over from a nearby marsh, and I spent hours watching them. I watched them while they dived elegantly between the plastic bags and I wrote everything down in my notebook. I always made sure I was back by the time they got home. I switched on the desk lamp, leaned my elbows on a book and pretended to read. Mum was very pleased, she saw the light under the door and said softly to her husband, 'He's still there, bent over his books.' He was pleased too, so pleased that one evening he even touched my hair, he said 'Here's a little man who's seeing sense at last!' I was pleased and not pleased. It was the fault of the budgerigars, that's for sure. They loved each other, I already had proof of that. But they hadn't decided to have babies. Every morning I went to the cage still in my pyjamas and there were no babies. I was starting to get uneasy. Budgerigars have no beard, no tits, you understand? They might be two females or worse, two young males. So the more the days went by the more worried I was getting.

When two people love each other they have babies. Mum had told me that just the week before. Mum and him too, of course.

It happened over dinner one night. That was the one time we were usually together. Anyway, while we are eating Mum touches her tummy, she touches it under the table and says, 'You'll be getting a little brother soon.' She says it just like that.

So I look at her because I don't understand a thing, I open my mouth and I say 'Why?' He answers me in a low voice, he says, 'Because when two people love each other they have babies.'

Do you see? It was right then that my budgerigars should have children. But no, that little brother was never born. One day Mum suddenly bent over, she went 'Ah!' and beneath her there was suddenly a pool of blood, it looked as if somebody had turned on a tap.

They got on, sure. Why would they have got married otherwise? Just that he was jealous. He thought that if all those years ago Mum had been with another man, she could forget herself and go with other men again. So sometimes he didn't come home at night. I mean, he came home but later. When he came back we were already in bed but we heard him anyway. He made a lot of noise, he slammed the door and anything else that got in his way. He paced up and down like a hungry wolf. He was looking for something to eat, us in other words, he wanted to devour us. I tried to ignore it, I don't know about Mum.

I repeated the names of the stones. You know? Even though I was taken up with birds now I could still remember all of them. Beryl, aragonite, pirite, quartz, pink quartz, fluorospar, opal . . . I went on like that almost the whole night.

Maybe it helped. Maybe it didn't. The next morning Mum had lost her baby.

Eighth Conversation

At last the babies were born. First the eggs of course and then a week later the chicks, little monsters with flesh-covered eyes and enormous beaks. Still, disgusting or not, I was sure at last that they loved each other, I knew which was the male and which the female. The first few days I was glued to the cage, I wrote down everything that happened in my notebook. One of the two was always sitting on the nest; while one got something to eat the other was keeping them warm. They really were caring parents. At the end of the first week their feathers started to sprout. The babies were nicer to look at now, they started opening their eyes, big black balls they were.

Them, no, I didn't tell them. I don't think they even noticed. We only saw each other in the evening at dinner and they spent most of the time talking about their own things. I heard their words of course but I tried not to listen, I was always thinking about something else. So Mum would say, 'Did you see? Number three hundred and twenty one had another haemorrhage,' and him, 'I've already stitched him up three times. There's nothing else to be done for him, his veins are rotten.' Or else the woman whose face was being eaten away by skin disease, she looked like a skull with a bit of flesh on it. She was pretty once, Mum said, I saw a photo, a lovely looking girl ... Or then again the man who arrived with his legs squashed by a lorry and the mother who when she was told her son was dead tried to kill herself in front of everybody. They were always talking about that kind of thing, about their work and I tried not to listen to them. I would think I wonder if that blackbird in the garden has made her nest yet? Was that little bird I saw a yellow tit or not?

But one day I got really cheesed off with it, so I slammed down my knife and fork and yelled 'Can't you two talk about anything else?'

I told you, didn't I? I've always had a horror of blood.

So neither of them say a word and they look at me. 'What is it,' he says, 'don't you like the work we do? Or perhaps', he goes on, 'our little ornithologist is frightened of blood, eh?' I'm chasing a pea round on the plate, so I don't look at anybody and I don't answer. But he doesn't stop there. He says, 'It's time you decided to grow up. Real men aren't afraid of anything. You have to get over your fears. Otherwise you get like a little girl. Do you want to be like a little girl, eh?'

Here we go, he was always going on and on like that. He was always saying that I wasn't to grow up weak, that I mustn't be in any way like my father, that even if I was born crooked, a bastard in other words, he would straighten me out. He wasn't doing it for my sake but for love of my mother who had this burden through no fault of her own.

Straighten me out how? Like pieces of iron, or trees. If I walked near him he would say, 'You're cutting across me, how dare you!' and he would land me one. If I slipped past him in the corridor, he would yell 'Are you trying to avoid me? Have you no guts?' and wham, another thump. All in all he put a lot of effort into straightening me out.

Mum was pleased. I think so anyway, because she watched and didn't say anything. She just smiled a bit like those Egyptian statues.

Sometimes I cried. I didn't understand a thing, what could I do? Then Mum would come up to me, she would stroke my hair and say 'You know, he's doing it for your own good, he loves you like your own father never did. When you grow up you'll see, you'll be grateful to him.'

Then I was even more confused than before. How could I be bad when he was so good?

The budgerigars never let their little ones get cold. They were always there with them and gave them something to eat every time they opened their beaks. Yes, I

wrote it all down in my notebook: in order to make
everything clearer, I even did some sketches.

Ninth Conversation

That business about blood, right. That day, strangely
enough, nothing happened at dinner, they left me alone
and they started talking about the hospital again.
Nothing happened that day nor the next nor the one
after. By now I was convinced I'd got away with it.

Then one morning, it was a Sunday, Mum had a work
shift and he comes in to wake me up whistling and he
says, 'Rise and shine, we're going fishing!'

Fishing was his great passion. He didn't like fishing in
the sea which was big and frightening but in small mountain streams. 'There's nothing like it', he would say, 'for
relaxing the nerves.'

So I get dressed, I pick up my white notebook and I
follow him out. After a couple of hours in the car we get
to an isolated valley. There's nobody around and the
stream makes a loud noise as it runs over the stones. He
says nothing most of the time and when he does say
something he's quite nice. When he's found the right spot
he gets out his rod and then he gets out a smaller one
and hands it to me. Then I say thank you but no, I
preferred not to fish because there must be so many
birds thereabouts, kingfishers, river blackbirds. All in all
I would be much happier sitting on a rock and doing
nothing. But he insists, he says come on, you can do both

at the same time, you can fish and watch the birds with no bother, all the better in fact because you have to keep absolutely still. This goes on a while, he says fish with me and I say thanks I'd rather not, then I see a glint in his eyes which I don't like and so I say yes.

He sorts out both the rods, attaches the fly, points out a place and says, 'You stand there' and he goes just a bit up river. From there he shouts, 'If you feel a tug, wind in the reel towards you as hard as you can!' Then he keeps quiet and I keep quiet too.

I'm just thinking that he's right, that it really is relaxing, when all of a sudden the rod almost leaps out of my hands. I just about hold onto it and as soon as it stops still I start winding the reel. He comes over to help, he stands behind me and pulls and after a short struggle an enormous trout comes out of the water. He says, 'Well done, you've done it!' and I'm pleased too. I'm pleased, I smile, until the fish waving in the air lands between us, at our feet. It's alive and shiny but its scales quickly go dull. It flaps about from one side to the other as if an electrical current were passing through it. It looks at me with one eye, then it jumps and looks at me with the other. Its pupil is small and black and a blade of grass has got stuck over it. So I think, it can see me but with a plank down the middle ... The metal hook is sticking out from behind its eye and there is blood all over the place. I turn my head and say, 'We can throw it back into the water now, right?' I say that and he grabs my chin with his hand and twists it. He answers, 'You know very well you catch fish to eat them.' At that point there's silence, I'm aware from its song that a thrush is flying nearby. As soon as she disappears he hands me a stone and says 'You kill it!' I don't say a word and drop the stone on the ground. He picks it up and hands it to me again. To cut a long story short, we go through this a few more times. He says quietly, 'Lord give me patience' but I'm sure he has less and less patience, in fact just a few minutes later I get a slap so hard that it knocks me down. From the ground I see him smash the stone down on the head of the fish, the head is reduced to a pulp with the hook still inside, at that point I think it's all over. As I'm about to get up he takes a knife out of his pocket, he takes it and cuts off the head. He comes over to me with the head in his hand, there's blood and yellow stuff dripping through his fingers, I don't realize what he's about to do. Anyway I get up but it's too late, he's already grabbed me by the neck, with his open hand he shoves the fish head into my face.

It must have been about midday. As we got back into the car he put an arm round my shoulders, he said, 'Does blood still scare you as much?' and he held me tight as if we were two schoolmates.

I couldn't wash my face until we were almost back in the city. We'd reached the outskirts when he stopped the car by a spring and said, 'Get out and rinse yourself off fast.'

I had a real job getting it off because by now my skin had absorbed practically all of it, it had gone deep down, right into my brain.

I said nothing to Mum and he kept quiet too. All he

said was 'Have you seen that fish?! Strange as it may seem, it was your son who caught it!' and he laughed.

Yes, I ate it together with them without saying a word. Only later I shut myself in the bathroom and stuck a finger down my throat as far as I could.

Tenth Conversation

Thinking back on it now I can tell you that that Sunday was like a baptism, a watershed. I couldn't say what it was exactly that happened, but I think time changed after that. Everything started to move faster. In some way which is not entirely clear to me, something began to slip out of my grasp.

The smell of blood, above all. It was still on me even though I washed. I couldn't sleep that night. I could still smell it there around my mouth, round my eyes. If I pushed my face into the pillow it seemed soaked with it. I turned my face upwards and I could taste it with my tongue, damp and sweet, round my lips. I felt horror and disgust but something else too. A bit like when there's a wind and you say, this wind is bringing something with it. Or else when you hear a musical tune and you can already tell from the first notes if it will make you happy or sad.

Well, that can happen in life too. It happened to me but it can happen to anybody. All of a sudden, the slightest thing can happen and you can be sucked into something else, pushed off course onto a path you've never seen before.

I don't know if that's clear, or if you see what I mean. I didn't know that time either. I know now, looking back, going backwards and forwards over everything in my mind. Baptism? No, rather an unction, something like the stench of death for hyenas.

Anyway, to keep to the story, the morning after that Sunday, even though I'd hardly slept at all, I get up to go to school and before getting dressed I go to see how my family of budgerigars is doing. At first I can't believe my eyes. I look and look again and as I look I say to myself, I'm still dreaming. Then Mum comes up behind me and touches me and I realize I'm awake and those murdered bodies on the bottom of the cage are my little chicks. One is on the right, the other two on the left near the feeder. All of them have a slash across the throat and down the stomach, among their little feathers you can see their inner organs quite clearly. They didn't die in the nest but away from it, yet they couldn't fly yet. Their parents ignore them, hopping from one perch to another and chirruping. How could it happen, I think, how could it? There I am by the cage unable to move a foot or even a finger. I'm still by the cage barefoot and in my pyjamas when he comes over with his coat on, peers through the bars of the cage and says, 'Well, they're dead!'

I didn't go to school that day. I said I was going but I didn't go. I took a bus as far as the sea, I walked up and down the shore-line until lunch-time. I was there, but I wasn't anywhere. For the first time, as clear as anything,

I had the impression I was made of wood. Of wood or stone, it doesn't matter; of something that doesn't feel if you touch it. Yes, I could have set fire to an arm and as the flames burned been completely indifferent to them. Only deep down there was a little bit still alive, a kind of ember which hadn't gone out, something which was there and which thought. It thought without me realizing it was thinking.

Like every other day I had lunch on my own. After eating I didn't know what to do, so I went to bed. I woke up all of a sudden, screaming, more or less as the sun was going down. This is what I was dreaming: I was walking along as I'd been walking along that day and suddenly, with no warning, I caught fire. The fire flared up from inside me. I jumped into the water but I couldn't put it out and so I screamed with all the breath in my body. I shouted not only in my dream but really. So with that scream in the room I woke up.

I stayed sitting at my desk until dinner-time. I only got up once to go into the kitchen. I went past the cage but I pretended not to see it. I could smell the blood, I was afraid to move the bodies. Then like every evening they came back by car. They parked in the garden and got out.

At the dinner table, sipping a glass of wine, he said, 'I hope you've thrown out those dead bodies.' I didn't say yes or no, I kept quiet. Then he got up and went to check. He came back in saying 'What are you waiting for, eh? For the worms to get them?' I stayed still, he grabbed me by an arm and tried to make me get up, I held on tight to the tablecloth and hooked my feet round

72

the legs of the table. He pulled but I didn't budge. The veins in his neck were standing out. Meantime Mum had served the soup, it was in front of me with green bits floating in it.

By then we'd reached this point, he was shouting, 'Move them!' and I was shouting, 'No!' it must have lasted a couple of minutes. Then I got up all of a sudden, catching him by surprise. I yelled 'You move them, murderer!' and I threw the plate with the soup in his face.

After that? After that I don't remember very clearly. My mother's shouting 'You're crazy!' and he's pushing my head in and out a basin full of water. In my room he locks the door. I remember that, the sound of the key. I'm on the floor and thumps and kicks rain down from every direction. I try to protect myself for a bit, then I get tired, it's useless and I pretend nothing is happening.

Later I'm in bed, or rather under it. I must have finished up there as in a lair. I can smell blood, I stick out my tongue, it's my nose bleeding. Blood all over the place. I told you; baptism or watershed.

The next day I was packed off to college.

Eleventh Conversation

Naturally I had to talk to a psychologist. You see, I have a certain amount of experience in your field too. To tell you the truth I didn't actually talk, it was him who tried to make me speak. Then, seeing I wouldn't open my mouth, he got me to do some little drawings. I scrawled something down and then went off to college. Perhaps if I had spoken or if I'd been more careful with the drawings I wouldn't have ended up there, but that's how it went and I left the same day. Was I happy? I don't know, that wasn't something I thought about. Probably yes, I was quite happy to be free of them. The only thing that worried me was interrupting my studies. I hadn't written anything in my notebook since the Sunday of the fish, I hadn't collected any stones or traced the movements of the birds. Then we left in such a hurry that I left all my notes at home.

The college was a big yellowish building with opaque glass. It rose out of the middle of the countryside. When I arrived the school year was already well under way and the boys all knew each other. The first day I was received by the Rector, a priest whose hair was all white and with damp hands as if he'd just dipped them in water. In his office he tells me some story about little sheep wandering all over the place with nobody to control them and about how nice it was to stay all together in the flock and how wise it was to use the stick. I understand next to nothing of all this and only later do I realize I'm running a high temperature. So I still don't see the other boys. I end up in the infirmary and stay there a good few days.

There's no one there apart from me. I spend the days huddled under the blankets and I stare at the wall opposite. I try to concentrate on my classifications for a bit, I repeat what I remember so as not to get out of practice but I'm very cold and I can't manage it. I begin to mix up names and shapes.

As soon as I'm better I join my dormitory and my class. There are so many rules there. I don't know them yet so I'm always getting things wrong and always getting punished. If I could have spoken with one of the other boys it would probably have been a bit better but we boys were not allowed to talk to each other. We could only talk at fixed times and under the eyes of the head teacher.

It's obvious why, isn't it? They were frightened we might get to like each other and it's a short step from liking each other to that other thing. I still didn't know such things existed, that one could go inside another even if they were both males. It goes without saying those things went on anyway. There was always a moment's opportunity at night or in the toilets. Did I like it? Didn't I like it? I don't know, I never asked myself.

The first time it just hurt. I was a bit surprised too, but then it just became a habit. What's more, because it was forbidden we spent the whole day thinking about nothing else. The first few months they did it to me and then I began to do it to others as well.

Now, if I have to define that period in words, two come into mind: cold and dark. Cold because the rooms and corridors were big and bare, dark because we never saw the sun and not even a bright light. When it comes down to it what we did was innocent. We did it to keep warm, to feel a bit of warmth inside.

Only when spring was well and truly under way did I

realize that the iciness had nothing to do with the air temperature. It was my skin that had become cold, and beneath that the flesh. Now and then I stopped to listen, occasionally it felt as if my heart had been changed into an icicle, that it was hanging there in my chest like a side of beef in a refrigerator.

No, they never came to see me, they'd never even sent me a change of clothes. Only once, after a couple of months, I got a postcard. On it was written 'I hope you're behaving yourself' and underneath the signature, Rita.

Anyway one day, not long before the end of the school year, they find us out. I was with a smaller boy and to tell the truth we were not up to anything really bad. I mean we were just holding each other's thing in our hands. Well as soon as the priest opens the door and the light catches us, the young boy starts to cry and yell that he's innocent, that I'd made him do it. They drag us off to another room by the neck. After a while the Father Superior arrives, he has a whip and straight away he makes the other one put his hands on the table and he hits them and hits them until they are nothing but strips of blood. Now and again he stops and checks to make sure I'm looking. Then he takes him to the door and before dismissing him he says, 'You've got your friend to thank for all this.' We are alone. I think now it's my turn and I steel myself, but nothing happens. He comes up to me, puts an arm round my shoulder and says, 'I'm sorry but you I have to lock up.' I think, well it could be worse. When he puts me in a dark room and locks the door I'm almost happy and breathe a sigh of relief.

It's funny but for the first time since being there I don't feel cold any more. The boy's hands come to mind, the blood dripping from them, and I can feel like a warm glow inside. We are not all iron and wood, then. Underneath, deep down there is still something hot and alive.

After a bit, since I don't know what else to do, I go to sleep. I don't know how much later it is when the sound of the lock wakes me up. I'm too slow to get up and then somebody pins me down and lies on top of me.

I catch a glimpse of the mask he's put over his face, a terrifying mask and in fact the first thing he says is 'Keep still, don't move because I'm the devil.' But as soon as his hands touch me I realize it's not the devil at all, they are damp and slippery like those of the Father Superior.

I don't have to spell it out, do I? You've got the point? I can only say that from that moment on the iciness came back and has never left me since.

A few days after they let me out of the room I ran off during a walk.

I took two days to get back to my own city. I walked part of the way, hitched a lift now and again. Along the way I convinced myself of one thing, that Mum knew all about it and was glad I was going home. Everything would go on as before, they would love me and that would be an end to it.

As I rang the bell, almost without realizing it I smiled. His car wasn't there, that made me more confident. I was still smiling as I climbed up the stairs and went into the kitchen. She was standing at the cooker, she turned round at the sound of my steps. I thought she was opening her arms. I said, 'Mum, I'm back!'

She said, 'So I see' and carried on cooking.

Twelfth Conversation

You want to know what happened next. What happened next was that I went straight back to college. Yes, they made a fuss about taking me back. They weren't willing to, they said that if you run away you don't go back. Mum pushed and pushed and in the end they gave in. I left two days later.

Those days at home were a bit strange. They didn't tell me off or anything, I was there but it was as if I wasn't there. They were neither pleased nor angry, as far as they were concerned I didn't exist and that was that. One morning while I was there in my room not really knowing what to do Mum came in and said, 'Sit down, I have to talk to you.' I sat down on the bed but I felt so cold I started to shake. I was shaking and my teeth were chattering. I wanted to tell her what had happened but I didn't have the nerve. I thought she wouldn't believe me, she would say 'You're a liar, you've made it all up.'

Anyway I sit down trembling and Mum says, 'You're doing it on purpose, you can't possibly be cold in this heat.' So I try to stop, I try but I can't. So to show I'm making an effort I open the cupboards and take out two jumpers which I put on. At that point she gives a big sigh. She sighs and says, 'You've no idea how difficult it is to be a parent,' then she rubs her stomach, looks at it and says, 'I have something to tell you, something important. Soon you're going to have a little brother.'

I take a good long look at her. To tell the truth you can't see anything yet. When she starts talking again I'm already far away – it's not me but the wooden me sitting opposite her and listening – I hear something like an echo in a mountain valley . . . that she's tired, she has so much to do, Daddy's tired too, he kills himself working all day, this new baby is on the way so it's better all round if I go back to the college like a good boy.

I don't say anything. I think, this is a story I've finished up in by mistake and I start shaking again like a leaf about to fall off a tree.

Sure, I've seen him too these past few days, we've eaten together a couple of times. The first time he pretended to ignore me, if he turned in my direction his gaze just slid off me. The second time, as soon as I sat down I got a bad dose of hiccups. Even if I held my mouth shut you could hear it. So after a bit he turns to me and says, 'You can pack that in now,' and as soon as he says it the hiccups get even louder. There's silence all around, that's the only noise to be heard in the room. Then he throws his knife and fork onto his plate, comes towards me, I curl up into a tiny ball, I'm trying to vanish into thin air but before he gets to me Mum gets up too, she brushes his arm and says, 'Please, no.' He stops in his tracks a minute then turns round and goes out of the house slamming the door.

I didn't see Mum after that. That evening she didn't

come to wish me goodnight in my bedroom and the next morning when I left the house I turned round to look up at the window but she wasn't there. Since I was travelling alone, I could have run away. To tell the truth it only occurred to me as I was getting on the train but I didn't have a penny in my pocket. Anyway, what would happen to me if I did? Just for once I wanted to try and be good.

If a baby brother was going to be born they loved each other, that much was sure. Yes, I hoped that that love would spread out like an oil stain. It would get bigger and bigger, so big that sooner or later I would slip inside it too.

All in all, it was better to wait so as not to spoil everything.

As soon as I got back they punished me. I wasn't allowed out for three months. Summer came and there were just ten of us left. In the meantime I'd failed my exams, I had a lot of studying to do and I had no time to think about anything else. I was always bent over my books, and I gave over any free hours to my classifications. It was a period in which I thought maybe not all was lost, that if I worked harder and harder I would still get to be a famous scientist.

The Father Superior? I met him face to face just a couple of times in the corridor. I would have liked to thump him, to shout that I knew who he really was. Instead, when he took my chin in his hand I only blushed and lowered my eyes.

It was autumn again, I passed my exams with flying colours. Nobody remembered to send me a parcel with

80

warm clothes. That was part of the punishment, not being able to phone home before Christmas.

Over those months the cold went deeper and deeper and started eating away at my bones. As I walked through the rooms during the day it was as if I could hear the sound of my thigh-bones, or maybe my shoulder blades. That sounds impossible, I know, but that's what it was like. They were turned to ice and rattled in my frozen flesh. Have you ever taken a fish out of the freezer? If you drop it on the table it makes a sound like a stone. That's what I was like over those months. I couldn't wait to get back to bed, under the tepid warmth of the blankets. But it was a useless wait because once I was in bed I was even colder than before. In the next bed was a small boy who cried all the time. So as not to hear him I thought about something else, about the hot, molten heart of the earth. In my mind I went down, layer after layer until I finally arrived there, in that hellish heat. It was a mass of flickering fire, as the earth moved round it rolled from side to side making terrifying whirlpools.

That image sometimes lasted into my dreams. Then instead of moving smoothly in its space, instead of staying there like the kernel in the middle of a piece of fruit, the mass of fire began thrashing furiously, thrashing and thrashing until finally it found something, a crack, a fissure, and came whooshing up to the surface. Up and up it came, the seas and lakes became liquid fire and the magma and lapillus came gushing out of the taps. Then, I don't know why, the same thing started happening to people. It wasn't the earth's heart that was exploding but their own, the one in the middle of their chest, and blood came pouring out of their eyes, their mouth, in long dribbles out of their fingers.

I always woke up at that point and as soon as I was awake I was cold again. Meantime the little boy next to me had managed to get to sleep; you couldn't hear him crying any more, there was only silence all around.

Just before Christmas at mealtime I got a telegram. I opened it by myself, in the toilet. It said: 'You have a little brother, his name is Benvenuto.'

Thirteenth Conversation

Where were we? When he was born? Yes, well, I didn't feel a thing when I read that message. How could I? I never saw Mum's belly or the two of them loving each other. All I thought was, let's hope he looks like me rather than his father, that he's nice.

Everything else was going along quite smoothly. There's nothing much to tell about that time. In the morning I had lessons, in the afternoon I studied. Once a week we all went out for a walk in the fields near the school building. They'd organized a football team but I refused to take part. I didn't like having to move, I much preferred staying in the classroom or studying in the library. I knew that I still had five years to go before being grown up, and I was putting all my effort into making that. I didn't talk to anyone any more. I only answered in class, when the teacher asked me a question. Why? I don't know, I had nothing to say.

As the months went by I began to feel as if I wasn't made of wood any more but I was a fruit that was drying out. I think that was because outside the classroom there was a persimmon tree. On sunny days I could see all of it, when it was foggy I could only see the fruit. First off there was the trunk with the branches, the leaves, the smooth round fruit, bright orange. Then bit by bit the leaves disappeared. From green they turned rust-coloured. Rust on the ground. The fruits were still there, brighter and brighter in colour.

Every morning I looked out and said, there we go, they've fallen down today, they're lying squashed on the ground amongst all the leaves. Instead every day they were still in place, they stayed up there getting smaller and smaller, redder and redder. They were shrivelling up, like I was inside. A voice told me that I had to go on, another told me I had no wish to go on at all.

Anyway, all this time there was no parcel from home with winter clothes in it. No parcel or any other news and I was dying of cold. So one day, when was it, February? I pluck up my courage and decide to call. Yes, I was allowed to by now. In fact I could have done it two months earlier. Why didn't I? I don't know, I didn't think about it and that was that. In any case, I finally decide to do it, I ask for some coins and wait for the right time, when I'm almost positive he won't be at home. There I am in the phone booth and while the receiver is going bleep bleep an icy sweat is dripping from my neck down over the whole of my back. I wait and wait and when

I'm finally just about to hang up a voice answers. I don't know why but it's him. Instead of being at the hospital he's at home. Well I steel myself to say who I am, I give my name. Who knows why I do that, perhaps I'm afraid that I won't be recognized just by the sound of my voice. I say who I am and he answers, 'Do you want to speak to your mother?' and of course I say 'Yes'. There's a moment's silence then his voice again. He says, your mother can't come to the phone, she's feeding our baby; here's what to do, call back another time and without another word he puts the phone down. I stand there for a moment with the phone in my hand. I hadn't thought of that either, that she might be feeding the baby. Instead of feeling warm I felt even colder.

That was the day some of the persimmon fruits start to fall off the tree. If I sit up straight at my desk I can see them spread around the tree trunk, scattered amongst the earth and the dead leaves like bloodstains.

What with one thing and another we get to Carnival. The last day, just before Lent.

There was a little party at the college and that day, or rather that night, something happens. We only heard about it the next morning. It was the gardener who found him just before seven o'clock. It was a boy a bit younger than me, a couple of times he'd asked me to help him with his homework. During the party he'd been one of the merriest ones, laughing with everybody, jumping about all over the place.

I didn't see the body. Only later in the courtyard I saw the red colour on the asphalt, the patch of guts. Not that they let us anywhere near it, of course, they were afraid

84

there might be some shark amongst us who when he saw blood wanted more. But as soon as I saw that patch I realized there was no question of him slipping or stumbling. He hadn't fallen but had leapt off. He'd come down like the persimmon fruits when they are fed up with being on the tree.

The next night I felt my legs, my arms, my stomach. How far had I gone? Outside I was dried up, withered, the lymph didn't circulate round there any more, I could have stuck a long needle in myself and not felt a thing. Only in some far off place, a long way away, was there something still moving. I don't know what sort of movement it was, maybe something that from being healthy was turning rotten. I got frightened, that's for sure.

Then a voice came. What voice? Always the same one, the one that speaks when I'm far off. That voice told me to go away, to run off somewhere safe because I wasn't brought into the world to finish up like a persimmon fruit. What was I thinking? I don't know, I just remember this: I saw before my eyes all the explorers, people who had left without knowing where they were going and then becoming famous. Did I want to sail off somewhere? Maybe.

When you have something in your head and all you think about is that in the end you manage to do it. Same with me and running away. Just a moment's lapse of attention during a walk was enough for me to disappear behind a bush and from there to take off across the fields as fast as my legs would carry me.

I never reached the sea. For three days I wandered round and round in the nearby woods. Then I was hungry, and cold. I reached a station and sat down in the waiting room. While I was sleeping there, stretched out on a bench, a man touches my shoulder and says, 'Have you got a ticket?' Of course, he was a policeman. Otherwise why would he have asked?

Fourteenth Conversation

Contrary to what I thought, nothing bad happened to me. They took me from the waiting room to an office. I waited nearly an hour, then a woman came and asked me lots of questions. For a moment I thought of making it all up. I looked at her face, I realized it was a waste of time, anyway all it would take was a couple of telephone calls and they would know everything. So I told her I left because I was fed up being in that place. I had a family, a little brother I had never seen, I wanted to be with them. The woman says nothing, she just writes everything down. When she's not clear about an answer she repeats it a couple of times, she puts it in different ways.

Then she says that's fine. She gets me to sign a piece of paper, she takes me into another room and disappears without another word.

At that point I had just one thought in my head. I wondered what they would do to me, if I would end up in prison or somewhere like that. I didn't have the faintest idea and I couldn't picture it. So I wait and I'm cold. I'm cold and I'm hungry too. Luckily a policeman comes and asks me if I want something to eat. I say yes, a sandwich, anything will do. I wait and wait and the sun goes down, evening comes. By now I'd thought of everything or nearly everything, there wasn't a prison harsh enough, they'd telephoned home and he'd said you can keep him, we don't want him back, he'd said it like when you buy something and it doesn't work. Or else they hadn't believed a word I'd said and they were hunting through photo after photo, file after file.

At one point I got sort of tired. Even if I thought and thought nothing happened. So I shut my eyes and rested my head back against the wall. The noise of the door woke me up. The woman from before came in and behind her my mother. I barely realized what was going on when she came rushing over to me and hugged me in her arms. In the middle of all that I could smell the perfume I used to smell when we slept together. Someone was speaking, it was her. She was saying, 'Since we heard from the college we've been so worried! Are you all right, darling?' As she said that she ran her hand over my hair my face my eyes, she touched me as if I was dead or as if she had never seen me.

After that we went into another room. She had to sign some papers, too. As soon as she finished she shook everybody's hand. She kept on saying, 'Thank you, thank you, I'll never be able to thank you enough.'

They've been nice, I told her. The woman who asked me all the questions even came with us as far as the main door, she stood there waving as we went down the steps.

At the corner a car was waiting for us. He was in it,

and with him my little brother. I got in and I didn't know
what to say, I was a bit frightened too. So as soon as I
saw that little bundle, I said 'Hey, how's it going?' The
little one was asleep. Perhaps he was scared, or he didn't
like my face. He opened his eyes and straight away
began howling like a madman.

My mother picked him up but she couldn't quieten
him. He drove with one hand on the gearstick, accelera-
ting too fast, not slowing down enough, his lips tight. It
took us two hours to get back home, he did the whole
journey like that. Even when the baby went back to
sleep neither Mum nor her husband opened their mouths.
I would like to have said something, I would like to have
said that the baby was cute and I was happy to be with
them, that I would always be good. I wanted to say that
but I didn't say it, my tongue didn't move. It seemed
fake, made of wood or glass.

A cartoon flashed into my mind. There was a shiny
round black bomb with a long fuse; the fuse was lit and
everybody had noticed it, nobody wanted to hold it, they
ran round in circles throwing the bomb to one another
until in the end it blew them all up.

Which was true? Mum's hug in the office or her silence
in the car? What was true and what wasn't? I asked
myself that question but I had no answer.

At home something had changed. My room had become
my little brother's room. There was a tiny little bed of
white wood with a teddy bear in it and a light which
moved and played a tune at the same time.

'You can sleep in the kitchen,' Mum said, 'the old camp-
bed must still be around somewhere' and without

another word and without looking at me she started
looking for it.

Fifteenth Conversation

At last I was back home again. It wasn't exactly the
place I'd wanted to go, but here I was. At that point I
thought everything would work out all right, how else
could it be? There you go, I'd forgotten the story of the
two cars.

Anyway I spend that night on the camp-bed. I sleep
really deeply, the sleep of an animal who's run away for
a long time. When I wake up the two of them are in the
kitchen, they're having breakfast. I keep my eyes closed,
I pretend I'm still asleep until they go out. Then I get
up and get dressed really slowly. I can't believe there
isn't a bell like at college which makes me do everything
in a hurry. I eat something from the fridge and then
start wandering around the house. I open cupboards,
drawers, I nose about everywhere. Naturally I was
looking for my own things here and there, my warm
clothes, my stone collection, the olive-green budgerigars.
I look and look but I can't find a thing. Or rather yes,
after a couple of hours I find the birdcage, the birds
aren't there any more, only a huge spider who has spun
a web between the bars.

They don't come back for lunch. The baby is at the
nursery. So I'm on my own until evening.

My mother is first back. She comes up the stairs with

89

the baby in her arms, I smile and go to meet her. I'm still smiling when she lays him on the table and changes his nappy. The baby looks around. Just when I think his eyes are looking at me, at my face, I smile even more. In fact I'm almost laughing. At that moment something happened which I would never have thought, he smiles back at me. While he is smiling and I'm answering him the doorbell rings and Mum goes to open it. So I bend over him and pick him up, he's soft, light as a feather and he's still laughing. So I have a good look at him and I see that yes, he looks like me, he has my mouth and my eyes and not his father's.

We're still there, laughing together, when those two come into the room. Mum looks at me and doesn't say anything. He sees me and yells, 'Don't touch him,' and he grabs the baby from my arms. The baby starts screaming straight away, he's all red in the face and screaming. I don't know what to do. I stand there with my hands in my pockets, perhaps I'm red in the face too, I'm ashamed and I don't know why. Then I go out of the room and down into the cellar. I wait down there until dinner-time.

I have a watch, sure. I got it years and years ago at my first communion. I look at it and when the small hand reaches eight I go up to the kitchen. They are already eating, they barely seem even to have noticed I've come in. I go up to the table to my place and I see there is no plate or glass, not even a knife and fork, nothing, only the white tablecloth.

What do I do? I stand there like a pole, I look at their plates, my empty place. I stand there a bit, then I say 'What about me?' I say that and nobody answers, they carry on eating perfectly calmly, their eyes on their food. I wait a bit more. When my mother serves up the next course I go. I go outside and look up at the lighted windows. As soon as the lights go out I move and wander round a bit. I haven't got the keys. Later, to get back in, I have to ring the bell. My mother opens the door, she's in her nightdress and dressing-gown. As soon as I'm up the stairs she says, 'Perhaps you were wondering why there was no place set for you at the table ...' To say yes I just move my head. Then she says, 'You should have stayed in college until June you know. Since you've gone and behaved so stupidly going off without asking our permission we're obliged to keep you at home. You're here but for us it's as if you weren't here, we're making out you're still at college. We can't do otherwise, that was the agreement. You were the one who went and broke it. It's for your own good you understand.'

I think she's joking of course. How could such a thing be true? So I nod my head, say goodnight, go to my bed and go to sleep.

It's only over the next few days that I realize that she meant it. Nobody says good morning or goodnight to me, nobody speaks to me. My place at table is always empty. What do I do? I spend as little time as possible there. I wander round the streets all day, I go home to eat, to eat something from the fridge. Where do I go? I don't remember, I move round the streets like a robot, a scarecrow. A couple of times I get a sudden urge to throw myself under a bus. That's what comes into my mind but my legs don't respond, so I just stand still. Sometimes, at lunch-time, I head for the schools. I stand there with my arms crossed and I watch the children come out as if I was a parent. When I see one come running out and hugging his mummy or daddy something in me moves all of a sudden, I feel like a lick of flame in my stomach. From my stomach it comes up to my eyes, I see red, I feel as if the hot, molten heart of the earth is inside me, as if it's exploded. Those were the moments in which just for a moment I was sure I wasn't yet dead.

Yes, I told you, to get something to eat I would open the fridge when they were out or asleep. I ate whatever I could find, whatever happened to be there. I didn't know it wasn't allowed. How was I supposed to know if nobody spoke to me? Anyway one night before going to bed I took some herrings in butter. To tell the truth I didn't care about feeding myself particularly. In fact I didn't care at all but you know how it is, instinct is the last thing to die, I almost didn't exist any more but my instinct did. Anyway reluctantly I eat this herring and lie down on my bed.

That evening he comes home late. He comes in and straight away opens the fridge. He stands there a moment with the fridge door open, then he shouts 'Who's eaten my herring?!' and he starts yelling. With my head under the covers I hear him going in to my mother and saying again at the top of his voice 'That bastard son of yours has eaten it! He's swallowed it down just to spite me!' I don't hear what she says. I don't know if she keeps dumb or if she answers quietly. Anyway he starts walking round the house smashing everything he can lay his hands on. What do I do? I get up, I run off, I hide in a cupboard. I knew he would come sooner or later. In fact from behind my door I hear him going into the kitchen. I hear him send the camp-bed flying with a kick, and yelling even louder he starts looking for me. I've only one hope, that he gets tired. But he's all fired up and in the space of less than five minutes he opens the cupboard and finds me.

I think: now I'll sick them up all over him. But he has the same thought. He sticks a spoon down my throat like doctors do and makes me throw up.

There we are facing each other, a pile of vomit between us. I have tears in my eyes from the struggle. He is panting. As soon as he gets his breath back he says 'Don't even dream about taking my things from the fridge!' and he gives me two slaps that almost send me crashing to the floor. That night I slept in the cupboard. I rolled myself up amongst the clothes like a fox in its lair in winter.

Over the following months nothing special happened. He was always a bit tense. When Mum couldn't see me I watched her without her knowing, I watched her and I got the impression that even if she pretended to be happy, inside she was sad. Meantime my little brother was getting bigger, he'd learnt to crawl. He could only go backwards. So when he saw something, he wanted to go up to it but instead he moved away from it. The further back he went, the louder he cried and the crosser he got.

I would like to have touched him, to hold him and feel his warmth but I couldn't. I wasn't allowed to, so I looked at him from a distance and that was all.

Just before summer my mother's husband started

getting even more restless. He was jealous again and every night he came home drunk. I hid myself wherever I could, I looked for a safe place even before dinner. I changed it every day so he couldn't find me. From there I could hear what he was shouting. He shouted, 'This one's just the same as the other one, a bastard! Bitch, cunt, whore, you'll spread your legs for anybody!'

That's what he said to Mum. I don't know what she said, I couldn't hear her, I was too far away. When she wasn't there because she was on night shift he would do the same thing with me. But I'd learnt to get away fast. I always wore trainers, I could run fast. He was drunk and almost never managed to catch me. In all those months he only caught me a couple of times. I was there under his feet and his blows didn't reach me. I mean, they were right on target but it was just as if they weren't because I wasn't there, I'd gone over to automatic pilot.

During the day as I wandered around the streets I was even more confused, when it came to eating and sleeping and speaking I didn't exist. I existed only at night, I existed only as a thing to release nervous tension.

You know the laws of electricity, don't you? If you charge up something and charge it up more and more in the end something happens, if it builds up too much it explodes.

So we get to the beginning of June. That's when something happens, Mum gets ill. I don't know what the matter was, the doctor came and even he couldn't tell us anything. In any case she lay there on her bed with her eyes closed like she was dead. When we're alone in the house I go to her door and I look at her. She doesn't see me. At least that's what I think until one morning she makes a sign with her hand for me to go over to her. So I go up to her, I go over to her bed on tiptoe. There I am next to her and I don't know what to say. She's silent too, but then she opens her eyes a bit. She gropes for my hand with her own, she finds it and squeezes it tight. What I notice is that her hand is freezing, colder even than mine.

My little brother? No, he wasn't there. At the first sign of illness they sent him into the country, to that aunt where I'd been too.

To cut a long story short, even though she was ill he didn't stop coming home drunk. The fact that she was in bed just seemed to make him even angrier. So every night I try and hide. He looks for me, he looks for Mum. He walks up and down yelling, breaking everything and so on. You can get used to anything, can't you? Even to that. After a bit it seems normal, just like anything else.

Then one night he comes back raging more than ever. Mum had been really bad that day. I hear him shouting from the street. He comes up the stairs, goes past my cupboard and straight into Mum's room. Sure, I listen, and after a bit, since I can't hear, I open the door of my hiding place. That's when I hear really clearly the shouts and the blows. I hear Mum's voice too, she sounds like she's whimpering or crying or about to cry.

You read things like that in the papers now and then, don't you? A weak, scared man who in extraordinary circumstances is swept up by superhuman strength, he's

95

capable of anything, he acts as if he wasn't himself but some mighty being.

That's what happened to me that night. Without realizing what was happening I thrust open the cupboard door, came out, went along the corridor with the tread of a lion and burst into their room with my muscles taut and my chest out. She was on the floor, he was standing over her with a knife in his hand. The only other thing I remember is going up to them and my mother shouting 'No!', the surprise in his eyes then all that blood splashing over me. But I don't remember the exact sequence of movements, or how the knife got from his hand to mine, from my hand to his stomach. Still holding onto the knife I leapt back and darted off even before realizing what had happened.

Down in the street I washed my hands in the first fountain I came across, I rubbed them hard for a long time under the water. The blood disappeared straight away but not the smell, that stayed inside me. As with the fish it had gone along some secret passageway, up from my fingers to some place between my nostrils and my brain.

I wandered around the city for a whole week. I went around at night mostly, I didn't read the papers, I didn't know if he was dead or not. It wasn't me moving but the automatic pilot, the beast whose guts had exploded.

Over those few days I struck four times.

They found the bodies of the first three almost straight away, they're still looking for the fourth. I waited for them all outside school. They were little more than kids, every time I went to wait outside a different school. I chose the ones who weren't being collected by anybody. I would go up to them discreetly, smiling, I told them I was a distant cousin, they followed me quite cheerfully and happily. I wanted them to be happy for ever.

I think you know everything about the first three, you've read the reports, haven't you? Strangulation, sodomy and so on. If you want you can send somebody to get the body of the fourth one. It must still be down there buried near the railway dump.

He was the youngest of all, seven or eight, no more, with a quiet, intelligent face. It was only with him, when he was lying in my arms and not breathing any more, than I got that urge. So without thinking I slashed his chest with my knife, it was tender, it opened up as if it was made of butter.

On the left of his chest was his heart, it was still moving.

Instead of tearing into it I lifted it out delicately as if it was a precious thing. With the last mouthful a great sense of calm and peace came over me, for the first time in all those years I felt warm.

They caught me just a few hours later. As soon as I saw that car I realized what was going on, they didn't have to chase me, I stood waiting for them, my hands in my pockets.

When I was already locked up inside here they told me that my mother's husband wasn't dead, I'd only given him a surface scratch.

Do you think if I'd known that before I might not have killed the others? Who can say? Can you?

Certainly I would have got off lightly. Do I regret

what I've done? Do I feel remorse? It doesn't make the slightest bit of difference, it was something inside me. Besides it's the same question as the two cars. Do they crash or don't they?

It depends what time they set off.

Beneath the Snow

Helsinki, 28 February 1969

Darling,

I'm in Finland for one of those endless conferences. It's gone on for three days and yesterday evening we had the farewell dinner for the participants. I didn't have the slightest desire to go, I pretended not to be feeling very well and went back to my room. I went from the conference room back to the hotel on foot. Even though it's March there is still a lot of snow around. Along the way I stopped a few times to look at the little wooden houses. It was dark and on the window-sills there were lots of candles shining. A colleague from here explained that it's a widespread custom in this country. That way during the winter you get the illusion that the days last longer. But I don't mind this early darkness at all. It's as if the brightly lit windows give off a feeling of tremendous intimacy. I've probably got that completely wrong, though. Who knows how many little hells are hidden away behind them! Still, walking through those empty silent streets I couldn't help feeling like Goldilocks, the little girl who creeps into the house belonging to the three bears. I would like to have gone in, drunk a glass of hot milk, snuggled down under a thick eiderdown and slept and slept without a thought in my head.

You know, there are lots of dreams it would be good to have. Dreams that you want really badly when you are awake but which never come when your eyes are closed. This is what I always dream about dreaming about. I'm walking along in a snowstorm, then I see a light coming from a house. I reach it, I go in. There's nobody there and it's very cosy and warm. I take off my clothes, put on a flannel nightgown and disappear into an enormous wooden bed under an eiderdown with little red hearts embroidered on it. I lie there wide awake. With my hands gripping the covers I listen to the snow falling. I hear the flakes dropping onto the roof one by one. I don't think about anything, I'm not waiting for anything. I breathe in and out. I'm happy like that and that's all. For a second I have the feeling not only that I can understand the world but that I am an integral part of it. A silent being among silent beings.

Yesterday evening, too, as I closed my eyes between the cold, anonymous sheets of the hotel, I whispered my desire for that dream.

I thought about it as hard as I could, and I was almost sure I would have it.

But I had another dream instead. I'd become really tiny and I found myself a prisoner in the doll's house I had when I was a little girl. It was a house on two floors made of light wood with doors and windows and lots of tiny furniture. Sitting at the lunch table was one of my

dolls. Looking out of the window I could see my room –
my shoes here and there, books open on the desk. But
everything looked as though it had long been left and
abandoned. I try to speak but no voice comes out. Suddenly I feel a tremendous cold inside me. So I reach my
little bed and climb up onto it. I don't know how long I
stay there but I know that as I lie there I hear a voice,
first quiet and then loud, the voice of a little boy.

Even though I can't make out the words, I realize he's
not talking but singing. He's singing a nursery rhyme.
Now and then he stops and laughs at something funny.
At that point I try to get up, to move an arm, a leg, and
at that point I realize I can't because I'm covered from
head to foot by a sheet of ice. I try to scream but the
ice smothers the scream. But it explodes inside the room
and with that scream I wake up.

I'm still in my dressing-gown, sitting at the small
writing table by the window. A young boy brought my
breakfast. After eating I felt a bit better. I looked at
my watch, I had four hours before I had to check in
at the airport terminal. So, barely aware of what I was
doing, I took some of the hotel's headed notepaper and
I did what I had never had the courage to do. I wrote
you a letter.

Rome, 1 March 1969

I've been back home two hours. I've unpacked my case
and put the dirty clothes in the wash. I made a cup of

tea and drank it in the sitting-room in front of the blank television screen. I should never have started writing that letter. It was a moment of weakness, of confusion. I'm a strong woman. At least that's what everybody thinks. Never a chink in the armour, nothing. Instead of which there was a weak spot and now I'm sure there will be no going back. It's a bit as if I'd turned on a tap: the water is running and I can't stop it any more. It's a banal comparison but I can't come up with a better one. Besides, originality has never been my strong suit.

I flew back with the director of the agency. I waited until we had taken off before telling him I was handing in my resignation. He thought I was joking. He said, laughing, 'That conference on meteotherapies has gone to your head.' I smiled, I said my head was still firmly on my shoulders. I knew what I was doing, I'd been thinking about it for a long time. My firmness alarmed him. He said, 'You're not starting to feel old, are you? You know, even if there are a lot of new girls you're still the best in the agency. Everybody's very fond of you, we all think very highly of you.'

I tried to explain my practical reasoning. I said, 'Now that my mother has died I don't need to work any more. She's left me enough to live on for the next hundred years without doing a thing.' Then I said I was tired, too, and I didn't want to go trailing round the world any more translating what people said.

At that point he said he understood. It wasn't unusual for women of my age to get a bit run down, but with some rest and a good holiday I would be right as rain.

'Why don't you go to Mexico?' he said finally. 'Apparently it's beautiful.'

I smiled, I touched his hand. Twenty years working together are a bit like a marriage. 'Alberto,' I said, 'from now on there's just one place I want to be and that place is home.'

He was silent for a moment, with a face like a worried child. Then, all of a sudden, he stared into my eyes. He said softly, 'So it's love?'

At that moment the plane was heading into an enormous cloud.

I thought about the letter. I replied, 'Yes, in a way it is.'

I look at my house, everything in order, perfect: the house everybody expects me to have. The furniture shows good taste, a few old pieces from my family, a modern kitchen. On the sitting-room table there are always fresh flowers, elegantly arranged. Coming back from long journeys this place always felt like a refuge. I had my little routines, the little habits of a person who lives alone.

Until last year my mother lived upstairs. It was usually me who went up. I would go up to see her after dinner. I checked that everything was all right and then I came back down to my own flat. Instead of being a pleasure those visits, being that close, weighed me down. Love. Perhaps that's exactly what was missing. When I was a little girl she looked after me and now that she was old, I was the one who saw to her. In all those years, though, there was never a gesture, not a single one, which might make me think it was anything more than a sense of obligation. I could have rebelled, certainly. But I should have done it long ago, almost at the beginning. What point was there in doing it now, when she was already old? How would that have changed my life? She was the one who had decided my life. I hadn't been able to do anything other than follow her lead. A guide dog for the blind, that's how I always felt, a calm and docile beast everybody could always depend on. Could I betray everybody's trust? No, I couldn't. Cowardice, you know, is something you pay for as you get older. Then you start thinking about all the things you could have done and didn't do. You start to see your safe and peaceful life as an uninterrupted sequence of loss and emptiness. So many things could have been but nothing was. A colourless slipping away of time and that's your lot. Now, I realize, love takes strength. You have to be brave in order to love. But nobody told me that when I was a child. I never saw my parents together unless they had some documents to sign. Love was what you read about in stories. A magic potion which the poor shepherdess gulps down, the kiss which wakes the sleeping beauty.

I often walk along the street and watch girls, young women. They are very different from when I was twenty. They make me feel envious. Girls from good families grew up to be good wives, they read edifying stories and believed them. Those months of my mother's illness, as she lay there with her eyes closed and her head lost in an enormous pillow, several times I was surprised to find myself hating her. These are things which shouldn't be said, but taps are like that, when you turn them on all sorts of things start coming out. I hated her stubborn high-handedness, I hated her for giving me life only to take it back again, day by day, drop by drop. How is it that you can hate an old woman on her last legs? You'll think me a monster. Perhaps that's what I am.

That's not for me to say. You'll be the judge of that when you've heard the whole story. All I can tell you is that the day she died I felt for the first time as if the air was reaching my lungs. I could breathe. Something had to change, that was all I could think. I wanted to break out of that circle which I always felt had imprisoned me. Many months went by before I decided. The morning I set out to see a private detective I felt as if I was walking differently, my step was bolder, my head higher. I thought, this is my first act of courage. Once I was back outside the door I thought the opposite. 'Emanuela,' I said to myself, 'that was no more than yet another in a whole string of acts of cowardice.'

I calmed down before long. When it came to it I'd only told him your date of birth, the first name of the midwife. It would be almost impossible for him to find you. Doubtless he would phone me after three months to say he was very sorry, there was no trace of you. I would say thanks just the same, I would pay his fee and without the slightest ripple I would go back to the same old life.

But that's not what happened.

The way I met him was as banal as you can imagine. I was coming out of school. I saw my tram going by over the road. I ran to catch it. As I ran I tripped, my books came loose and went flying onto the pavement. Before I could work out if I'd hurt myself or not, I saw his hand stretched out. He took my arm, picked me up. Once I was on my feet he asked, 'You all right?' and from my feet to my head his gaze took in my whole body. I took a quick look at him, he was young, he was wearing the uniform of the Allied soldiers. I said, 'I'm absolutely fine, thank you.' I bent down to pick up my books. He beat me to it, picked them up and handed them to me. I thanked him and said, 'I have to go now, it's late.' He insisted on coming with me. I said, 'No, thank you, it's fine, I can manage.'

He came with me anyway. Along the road he told me something about himself. He was a medical officer, he'd been in Italy just over a year but he felt as if he's always been there. His grandparents were Italian, from Lecco, did I know it? Perhaps that was why he felt so at home and why he'd picked up the language before anyone else. I didn't tell him anything about myself, I knew it wasn't right. When we were a couple of blocks from home I told him I'd arrived. 'Where do you live?' he asked me. I pointed vaguely with my hand, over there I said.

He pretended to believe me and stopped. 'Goodbye then,' he said. I said goodbye too and went on my way. I didn't look round until I got to the corner. He hadn't moved an inch. As soon as our eyes met he smiled. His teeth were white and perfect. He was tall, strong and he had a kind look like Gary Cooper.

When I saw him outside the school next day I didn't try to avoid him. I went up to him, smiling, as if I already knew he would be there. He had a flower in his hand.

As soon as I'd reached him he kissed me on the forehead. I started to tell him about myself. I talked and talked and as I talked my cheeks were burning. I started thinking about him when I was on my own, too. I would think about him and smile. Before going to sleep I would hug the cushion as if it were him. I'd read several novels for young girls. I knew this was love. It had hit me when I was least expecting it. The novels said it would be like that. I was already thinking about the future. In my mind's eye I saw a little cottage with a front lawn and apple-pie cooling on the window-ledge. He had a huge car, almost like a van. In the evening he would come home exhausted from the hospital and I would cook his dinner. He would tell me about the patients he was treating and I would listen. I was proud of him, of his human generosity. After three years we already had two children. They had red hair and freckles. We would have more too, as many as came along. We still loved each other like when we first met. We were happy and it was as simple as that.

After a month he asked me to go out with him one Sunday afternoon. I told my parents some story about an extra maths lesson at a friend's house. My friend knew everything of course, she was in on it.

We went to the cinema. My heart was beating in my throat and I couldn't follow the thread of the story. Soon after the beginning of the second half he drew me gently to him and kissed me. I was surprised by his tongue, I didn't know you could do that with it too. From the moment of that first kiss time began to speed up for me. I wanted to leave school straight away, tell my parents, set off at once for America. I never discussed these plans with him, though. I don't know why, I was scared. He was thirty, I was sixteen. Some nights I couldn't get to sleep. I thought maybe he's already got a family and he hasn't told me. One day I saw a postcard with an American stamp sticking out of his jacket pocket. I couldn't read what was written but the writing was a woman's. But still I didn't ask him anything. When he held me close and looked into my eyes and said sweet things, all my suspicions disappeared, melted away. Yes, he was as much in love with me as I was with him.

For several months my parents didn't notice anything. They only began to get suspicious when I started getting bad marks at school.

I hung on to my secret though. I would reveal everything just before leaving for America, when the wedding was about to take place. I was almost sure they wouldn't agree to it but I was equally sure that as soon as they met him, any resistance would vanish.

I was naïve, don't you think? Perhaps a bit ridiculous even. I hesitated before telling you this part of the story. Then I decided it was better you should know. Even if I don't come out of it too well I wanted you to know that you were a love child. Or at least, a child of what I thought was love.

It happened six months after we first met. I was expecting my period but it didn't come. I waited another month before telling him. At first I thought it might just be late. I told him one Sunday afternoon as we were walking around the empty streets. I had imagined that moment so many times. I was sure that he would laugh, that he would lift me up in his arms with a hug. Instead, as soon as I'd said the last word – the last word was child – he stopped dead in his tracks. He looked at me without a word, then he scratched his chin. He said, 'Really?' I replied I was almost certain but at that point I felt like crying. He saw to the tests. He read the result and told me what it was. It was true, I was expecting a child. He didn't show up the next few days, he disappeared for over a week. In the end I was the one who went to his boarding-house. I waited for him, leaning against the railing for hour after hour. When he saw me he gave a start, he looked annoyed. I burst into tears, I couldn't hold them back. He put an arm round my shoulders. 'Come on,' he said, 'don't do that, not here.'

We went to a bar, he bought me a camomile tea. As I was blowing on it to cool it down he told me he'd been called back to his own country. I wasn't to worry, though. As soon as possible he would sort out the marriage papers, he would send a ticket so I could join him over there in Oregon. I listened to him and I could hardly believe it. It was as if without noticing I'd slipped into a film. With a tiny voice I asked him to come and meet my parents, to explain everything to them. He nodded, he said that if he had time he would call by at my house one of those days. Then he got up. His chair scraped along the floor. He said, 'I really have to go now.' I clutched at his sleeve, I asked for his address. He scribbled something on the back of an envelope and gave it to me. Before leaving he gave me a quick kiss on the forehead.

I can still see him. I can see his khaki jacket and trousers, his legs moving off with their elastic step.

I don't know when he left exactly. I waited for twelve days and there was no sign of him. I telephoned the barracks from a public phone booth. They told me he'd left with the last contingent. I hung up without asking anything else.

Yet I still wasn't desperate. I trusted him. I thought everything he'd told me was true. That's what heroines in novels were like, you know, they were optimistic to the last, they faced up to their troubles sure that in the end everything would work out for the best. Just the month before I'd gone with him to see *Gone with the Wind*.

So that evening, before going to sleep, I said what Scarlett O'Hara had said. After all, tomorrow is another day. The next morning, instead of going to school I went to a bar and wrote him a letter. Using the most flowery language I knew, I told him how I imagined our future life together. I didn't even mention the most urgent thing. I fooled myself inside that everything was already settled.

I waited more than a month for an answer. One morning it arrived. It wasn't his letter, though, but mine, stamped all over: Address unknown.

It was then and only then that everything fell to pieces around me. Everything, but not you. You carried on growing inside me and it was no longer possible to keep you hidden.

I imagined escaping. I imagined that for shame they, my parents, would send me away. I saw myself wandering from door to door like the little matchgirl, begging something to eat. I imagined all sorts of terrible things lying in wait for me, and me facing up to them with my head held high. But none of all that happened. They heard my news in grim silence. Then my father said, 'Get up and go to your room.' As soon as I was alone I fell to my knees at the foot of the bed. I prayed, I thanked God for my parents' goodness.

Now I know that that was the worst thing of all, but at the time I felt lucky. It was like grace raining down from heaven.

The next day my mother called me into the sitting-room. She said that first of all I would leave school, I could tell them I had nervous exhaustion. Then she and I together would go to our house in the country where we would wait for the baby to be born, far away from prying eyes. I couldn't hold back my emotion. I kissed my mother, I said thank you thank you Mummy. She sighed, looked at my belly which by now you couldn't miss, and said, 'If you hadn't waited so long to tell us we could have sorted it out far better than this.' Then I was happy I hadn't told her before. Not even in my most desperate moments did it occur to me to have an abortion. I'd got hold of a book on pregnancy almost straight away. I knew what was happening to you day by day. Little stumps of arms and legs had already appeared, your head was already a fair size; from these stumps tiny hands had sprouted, tiny feet, they had fingers and toes which were small and perfect, the nails would appear later. How could I suck you out, toss you in a basin on the table? Not even my growing resentment towards your father could have led me to do something like that. I could remember the moment in which we'd conceived you. We'd loved each other in that moment. It doesn't matter that it lasted no more than a fraction of a second. You were the extension of that second. A second that lasted a whole lifetime. I would love you, I would even manage to love the fact that you would look like your father. For a tender memory, not for anything else.

So with these thoughts in mind, I set off for the stay in the country.

In those months, apart from my mother I saw nobody. We were both quite calm. I went for long walks in the garden. I looked at the flowers, the bees squatting on them. I felt as if I was part of nature too, and that feeling gave me a great inner strength. When we were on our own I often used to talk to you. In our conversations I called you Riccardo. I was sure you were a boy. I'd given you that name because of my passion for the Knights of the Round Table. Richard Lionheart.

At the end of the seventh month, I began to make you a little suit which I hid from my mother. I crocheted it and the wool was blue. It took me more than forty days to finish it. I wasn't used to that kind of work. When I'd sewn the last seam I showed it triumphantly to my mother. She looked at it in silence, the corners of her mouth turned down. Over her silence I exclaimed, 'Now that I've learned how I'll make at least ten of them!'

Then she was the one to speak, she said 'You'll be wasting your time because you'll not even lay eyes on the baby.'

112

I didn't understand right away, only when she talked about my being under-age and the necessary papers. I would sign a legal document and give up the child even before bringing him into the world.

Did I rebel? In my own way, as far as I was capable. I burst into sobs and my mother consoled me. Between my tears I said that if they didn't want anything to do with us I would go away and work, if they didn't want the shame I would take my baby and disappear for ever. She tried to make me see reason. Neither of them wished me any harm, they only wanted to do what was best for me. It had been an accident and it would be dealt with like an accident. They couldn't let me ruin my whole life because of one moment's carelessness. I was young, pretty, intelligent, from a good family. In that state, with a child, how would I ever find a husband? I had to think of the future and not of one unfortunate slip-up. The child would be better off in a real family, I would be better off without him. I still protested. I carried on protesting until she said there was no point, I was just upsetting myself to no purpose. I was a minor and thanks to the law they were to decide for me. There was nothing else to be said. One day, when I grew up, I would understand.

There was barely a month to go before you were born. I passed it in absolute silence. I prayed, I turned to the Madonna. I said, 'Mother of all men, in your infinite goodness, protect me.' I was hoping for a miracle, that he would come back.

But labour pains arrived before any miracle. You were

the right way round and the right size. Yet according to the doctor he had hardly ever seen such a long and difficult labour. I wasn't frightened of the pain, I was frightened of losing you. Instead of pushing I held on to you. I knew it was dangerous for both of us, it was a risk I wanted to take. To die together, at the same moment. But nature is powerful, she programmes life to perfection. Out you came into the world. You were a healthy baby boy. The midwife wrapped you up in a sheet and disappeared with you in her arms into the next room. I caught a glimpse of you, I saw your head, you had red hair.

A year's sluggish apathy followed that morning. I went back to the city but I didn't take any interest in anything, I didn't speak, if I looked around I didn't see anything. Two months later, following the advice of the family doctor, I was sent to a Swiss clinic. I remember very little about that time. A colour, white, no face and no clear sound. I spent my time sleeping, talking silently with you. I would say, 'Come on, give your mummy a nice smile' and all those other things which mothers say to their babies. I tickled your tummy, I kissed your chubby feet. Holding you in my arms I spent hour after hour at the window. It was snowing. Little birds with their feathers fluffed up hopped over the lawn looking for seeds, I pointed them out to you. Then came the thaw. Patches of earth started to appear in the garden below, the first snowdrops. Then something happened inside me, too.

I don't know what exactly. For some unknown reason I decided not to look behind me any more. The only feeling I was aware of was a stunted goodwill. The doctors were satisfied with that. Before Easter I was back in Milan, I studied privately and took my exams.

If you've been told that you're not the son of the people who've brought you up, perhaps you've imagined some exciting adventure for your real mother, on the margins of the law maybe. You'll be disappointed to find out that your mother is part of the common crowd, one of those ladies with the neat suit and straight back that you meet in the street or on the bus.

These days there are a lot of student protests around the city. They roam the streets in large groups shouting, down with bourgeois society! Perhaps you are there, too, perhaps you've seen me pass by with my dark blue raincoat and my handbag and you've looked at me with contempt.

But the human soul, you know, is more complicated than the clothes we wear, than the way we look.

If I had the courage, if I wasn't afraid of looking ridiculous, I would tear my clothes off, I would climb up on those barricades and shout alongside you. What unites and divides us is our sense of pain, not our parka jackets or our overcoats. For the most trivial of reasons, because of what's done or what people will say, I've been forced to live a life that is a fake. That's what we have to free ourselves from, from hypocrisy, from barriers. That's why the violence of these young people fills me with horror, they seem blind to me, ready to exchange one lie for another.

If you'd been with me these past days who knows how we might have fought! But that would have been good,

115

too. It would have helped both of us to grow just a bit more.

The only thing of yours I have is the little blue suit I made for you in the country. I keep it in a drawer in the cupboard. The nights I can't get to sleep – and there are many – I get up and turn it over in my hands. It's odd, but even though you've never had it on, it still has the smell of a newborn baby. The smell of milk, of wee-wee, of talcum powder.

I imagine that by now you've had enough of all this. You'll be thinking, what does this old woman come bothering me for? Or you'll be wondering how it is I came to understand so many things and didn't do anything about them. I've often wondered that, too, and rather than any answer all I have is a feeling. I don't know if it's ever happened to you, but walking over the fields sometimes in spring you come across tapering, opaque wrappings – empty snake-skins. There you have the whole body, exactly the right size with spaces where its eyes go, only there's no live animal inside it any more, no heart, lungs, or poisonous fangs. It's all gone. Well, from the day you were born that's just how I've felt, as if I had nothing inside any more. On the outside I was the same polite, attractive girl as ever, but on the inside my guts, with all their power of feeling, had dissolved. I felt like a robot. I was one. I am one. It's just that in some corner of me I haven't been able to spot, my capacity for seeing has remained intact. I've watched the lives of others the way a director watches rehearsals from the stalls. I've watched, I've judged, I've formed my own opinions about the world. Perhaps I've been able to understand some things better and more clearly than other people because I've always stood apart. All in all, if you look at how I live and what I think, I'm a sensible person. This is one of the things I wanted to tell you. Beware of good sense! Life is anything but sensible. Life is constant movement, instability. To get by in it you need to be elastic, open, not tied to anything. As long as you are in good health, good sense is nothing but a siding which you shunt up and down. You know the scenery off by heart. You know how the journey begins and how it ends and because you know that you fool yourself into thinking you are strong and calm. But what if you change track, if you start going through different countryside? That's the point.

I told you that all these years my body has been nothing but an empty skin, a paper bag. That's true but it's partly not true.

Every year, in fact, in exactly the same month as I conceived you, my stomach would slowly start to swell up, as if there was something inside. After a month I would start getting sick, my energy would flag. After nine months a searing pain, just as when you were born. Then everything would return to normal. The first few times I naturally went to the doctor. It's ridiculous, but I had an idea that maybe what was happening to me was something like what had happened to the Madonna, that I had conceived a baby through some higher intercession. It could have happened at a time when I was befuddled, at a time which I couldn't remember anything about. Instead of which they were just phantom pregnancies. I got used to that too. At the office my colleagues would say to me, 'It's impossible, you eat like a bird and yet

117

you're putting on weight!' They advised me to go to a doctor, to get my hormone levels checked. In the street now and again somebody would congratulate me as they passed me by, and then I would hurry along without looking anyone in the face. Year after year, for twenty-five years, a part of me that was still alive carried on that ritual. Then came the hot flushes, the sudden and violent crying fits. I'd reached the menopause. At that point I thought, it's all over at last.

In the meantime, my mother had died after a long illness. My father had passed away even before I finished studying. I thought I was about to start a new chapter in my life, a sad, shabby chapter but one which was at least mine. I signed up for a course on ikebana and on Sunday afternoons I had tea with my colleagues.

Instead of which in spring, the same as every year, my stomach started to swell up. I didn't feel drained this time but my stomach swelled up like all the other times. Then I understood what it was. It was a punishment, the price of my cowardice, which I would continue to pay to the end of my days.

It was only when on the usual date there was no change in the size of my stomach that I began to get worried. I'd gone to that private detective the month before. Rationally I don't know why I did it. Perhaps I knew something was going to happen. Perhaps it was my desire to put an end to my endless punishment by having a face before me. I didn't want to turn up and upset you by claiming my non-existent rights.

All I wanted was to know how you had turned out, who you looked like, where you lived.

But when two months after the birth date I felt an almost unbearable pain inside, I went to a doctor. The irony of fate, it was the same day as the detective gave me an answer. You existed. Your father was an engineer, your mother a French teacher. You were studying medicine, you lived two streets away from me.

A week later the doctor answered too. 'I'm sorry,' he said, 'but inside you have a tumour almost the size of a baby.'

All those months it had never even crossed my mind that it might be that. Yet when the doctor told me I wasn't in the least surprised. For more than twenty years I'd wanted something to grow inside my stomach and in the end my wish had been granted. With one small difference. Instead of nourishing a life inside me, I was harbouring death.

'If you had come to see me before ...' the doctor had said with a sorrowful look. I'd shrugged as if to say never mind. But then – it was part of his job – he threw me a life-line. I was to have an operation straight away to stop the crazed cells spreading all over my body. He gave me a piece of paper with the test results. I said yes, that would be fine. In fact I didn't care one way or the other.

A lot of people go sort of mad when they are told they are about to die. They cry, they sink into despair, they spend all their money living it up. Others suddenly get converted, they find their final strength in faith. Nothing of the kind happened to me. Even the doctor was surpised. The news put me into a kind of euphoria.

119

On the way home I stopped at a plant shop. I spent the whole afternoon absorbed in making the arrangement. For the first time I didn't do it the way I was taught in class. I arranged the dried logs, the moss, the lichen, and over all of it trailed a long branch of dog roses. I picked the scarlet juniper berries off their stem and half hid them between the moss and the earth.

I was so absorbed by this study of shapes and colours that I forgot to have dinner. Finally satisfied, I looked at it from every corner of the room. Yes, it really was a perfect ikebana. Perfect not because it followed all the rules but because at last it expressed what I had inside.

I baptized it 'Beneath the snow'.

Over the next few days I did the necessary tests. Then, as if there were nothing wrong, I set off for that conference in Helsinki. There, who knows why – because of the snow? or the silence perhaps? – I started writing you this letter. Do I regret it? No, it's done me good and that's enough. Tomorrow I'm going into the clinic for the operation.

When I got back from Finland – why am I only telling you this now? – I couldn't resist it, I came to see you. Making some excuse or other I asked the janitor which was your window. Checking my watch now and then as if I had an appointment, I walked up and down below for the whole afternoon. It was only towards five o'clock that I saw a fleeting shadow behind a curtain.

Still here, darling. Still alive and with you still inside.
The crazy cell baby has put his shoots all over my body,
colonizing my liver and then my brain. They heard I was
ill at the agency. Alberto came to see me in hospital. He
couldn't hide his astonishment. He kept on saying, 'I
can't believe it, you were so well . . .' Of course he knew
nothing about you. Apart from my mother and my father,
nobody ever knew.

If you could see me now you wouldn't believe I was
your mother but a mad old woman. You must have
thought that too the other day, when you came out of
your house and saw me sitting on a bench opposite. Our
eyes met almost by mistake and straight away you curled
your lip and looked the other way. You're right, my hair
has almost disappeared and the skin lies over my skull
like an old, yellowed piece of wrapping paper. I wanted
to grab hold of you, hug you tight, feel the life flooding
through your body. Instead of which I looked down, pretending I'd lost something, and I shuffled my feet in the
dust.

I don't see anybody any more, and none of the few
people I know come to see me. When death has so obviously taken hold of a body it's frightening for everyone.
I refused to go into hospital before my time was up. I
hate all that messy business with wires and tubes, having
operation after operation. Why spin out a life for a few
more days when it has almost gone anyway? Once, when
I was a teenager and when I still understood poetry, I
read a Hungarian poet. I don't remember how it started

121

but I remember it finished like this: 'I lived uselessly / and even death will be a vain thing.' That's in my mind all the time now.

In order to see you without your spotting me I've started to bring plastic bags with me. I stop under your window and I feed the cats. I've made up names for all of them. When they all come together I call them my children. I notice how embarrassed the doorkeeper looks. She obviously thinks Miss M. has gone off her head. Along the road I see people looking at my hair, but instead of irritating me it makes me happy. All my good sense has been blown away in a single puff! Soon I won't exist any more. What do I care about anything else? If I were sensible I'd give you my last words now, the important, beautiful ones that mark off a whole life. But all I can do is laugh. Perhaps the crazed cells are at work in my brain? Who knows.

Last night I had a dream. I had *that* dream. I was walking for hour after hour in a snowstorm. At each step I sank in up to my knees. When I saw the light in the distance I could already feel the quiet torpor of frostbite creeping up. I gritted my teeth and found the strength somewhere. I fell against the door like a dead weight, it wasn't closed but only ajar, it opened. Inside, the fire was lit, there was wine and a meal on the table. I ate, I drank. Then I went upstairs, the bed was ready, a white flannel nightgown was folded on the pillow. When I'd put it on I disappeared under the feather quilt. Beside me a candle was burning, the storm was still raging outside. With my eyes open I began counting the snowflakes, the ones that landed on the roof and the ones that got stuck on the window-sill. Then I began to see all those which landed on the forest round about, on the tips and the branches of the trees, on the earth. I finished up under the white thickness. I broke the crust of the ice, I went further down where you find the acorns, the seeds, the humours ready to awaken in spring. I saw the snakes asleep wrapped round each other and the frogs stretched out with their legs apart as if they were dead. I don't know what I was, perhaps a worm or an ant. I moved nimbly down there. I was in the bed and I wasn't, I was there and everywhere. I was breathing. All of a sudden the candle went out and I went to sleep. I slept and I dreamed about sleeping. It was only then I understood.

When I got up this morning I was very weak. I struggled to open the cupboard, I pulled out the little blue suit, I ironed it and wrapped it first in flowered paper and then in strong brown wrapping paper. I checked in my bag to see if I had two bus tickets. I chose a post office some way away, I made up a name and an address for the sender.

The woman at the post office window asked me if there was a letter inside, I said, 'No, no letter.' Then she threw it onto the parcel scales. As she dropped it she saw me jump, she asked me in an alarmed voice, 'Is it fragile?'

In the faintest of voices I answered, 'Very fragile indeed.'

For Solo Voice

Yesterday the television people came. I'd been waiting for them since two o'clock, they turned up just before four. There were six of them altogether. As soon as they came in they started hunting around for the sockets. While they were setting up the camera in front of my armchair I told the interviewer that this was the first time I'd appeared on television. Were they positive I should speak? Was it really me they wanted? She reassured me, she said I was to talk as if the camera wasn't there at all. In the meantime the men were still fiddling around and each time they moved an armchair or a book it would make me jump. Not for the things themselves, but because of the dirt underneath. You know how I live, all the dust there is around here, how could I explain to them that I am not very strong and I have no one to help me with the house-cleaning? You are young and all this will just make you laugh, it's silly, isn't it? I was very embarrassed though. Blame my old-fashioned upbringing. Never mind. So when they switched on the lights I asked them to focus just on my face and not on anything in the room, the books or my husband's statues. Then I asked, 'Is this going out live?' They laughed. No, it will be broadcast in three months' time, maybe four. If there's something I don't like I can tell them and they will cut it out. Can you check whether that's true? That's what they said, but I'm not sure I believe it.

Half an hour later they were ready for the interview. One of the men tapped a board, he shouted, 'The survivors, take one' and the videocamera started. The journalist was sitting opposite me. Still smiling she said my name, my surname, and widening her smile even more she asked me, 'Could you tell us your story?' At first my voice was a bit shaky, then bit by bit it became almost normal.

I talked about my childhood, about life in my city during the Great War. I talked about my father, my mother, their backgrounds. I told them how I met my husband and about the start of the persecutions. I spoke very well, you know, very calmly, I didn't think I could do that. I spoke as if it wasn't my story but somebody else's. I didn't notice how the time was passing, the interviewer was still smiling, nodding her head and she seemed satisfied. I carried on talking, about the birth of my daughter, our difficult relationship. Just as I was talking about her death, the journalist interrupted me for the first time. 'When did that happen?' she asked.

So in my head I counted how many summers had passed, I counted and as soon as I had counted I forgot, I started again from scratch but just as it was clear in my mind it slipped away again before getting from my brain to my tongue. I don't know how much time went by, the interviewer didn't seem bothered but I was, I was and as the minutes went by I got more and more upset.

It was that interruption that was at the root of it all. I wasn't expecting it, you see, I lost my thread. That's what age does for you. I hunted around for something to say to get me going again but my head felt empty. The camera was still rolling, you could hear the noise in the room, that was the only sound to be heard. After a bit the interviewer tried to help me by coming in again.

She said, 'Your mother died in tragic circumstances too, didn't she? Could you tell us what happened to her?'

She caught me by surprise, I wasn't thinking about my mother at that moment but a whole lot of other things. Instead of my mother I saw before me the kitchen teapot furred on the inside. I put the teapot from my mind, I said, 'She's dead . . .' and in front of me appeared my window geranium, all yellow and shrivelled because it's over three years since I repotted it, I pushed that image aside too and everything began to get blurred. You know what it's like when as a child you are playing and you spin round and round with your eyes closed, you spin round faster and faster and then you stop, you open your eyes and everything is still spinning round you, you don't know where you are, like Tom Thumb in the wood, something like that, that's what happened to me, I was breathing hard, I didn't know where I was any more.

At that moment the journalist asked me the same question again. Of course she already knew the answer, she was asking for the viewers who didn't know the story, she said, 'When your mother passed away she was in hospital, wasn't she?'

Then the cork burst out of the bottle, everything came up into my mouth, my eyes. I shouted, 'I don't know!' and I started crying. I saw my mother's face between the sheets, her dried-up body, I saw it not like now when I'm telling you about it but as if I were right there, at the very moment it happened. I hadn't cried, I hadn't even cried in years after, I tried not to remember it, but all of a sudden almost seventy years on there she was in front of me, she was in her bed then the bed was empty and unmade and a closed lorry of Germans was leaving before my very eyes. By now I was creaking inside like an old boat. I'm quite familiar with these senile bouts of sentiment. I wonder why it is that as you get older you cry more and more, you start and you can't stop, you go on for hour after hour and nothing can console you. Your heart is weaker, more vulnerable, your eyelids start to sag. You only stop when you sleep. That's what happened to me yesterday. Even now, telling you about it, I'm ashamed, I can feel myself blushing.

The journalist froze, sitting bolt upright with her notes in her hand, and you could still hear the noise of the videocamera in the room. I thought they had turned it off but they hadn't, they were all standing there as if hypnotized by a snake. Meantime I was crying even more, sobbing, I was crying for my mother, crying because I couldn't stop crying, crying because I was crying and they were filming me. Still crying I gestured no with my finger, I have bad legs you know, I couldn't get up and go into another room, I gestured no but it didn't do any good, so I hid my face in my hands, they made a shell over my face, the tears leaked out underneath, I could feel their warmth on my breast, my jumper was getting soaked, I thought right, that's enough, I gathered my last ounce of strength and concentrated everything on one point, my tongue, I opened my mouth and with all the breath in my body I shouted, 'There's no more butter in the fridge!'

It was only then that they stirred, they stopped the machine.

When they left I was still crying, I cried all night. Do you think there's any way of stopping them? You know all sorts of people in that business, can you find out? I can't settle any more, I can't sleep. That's another thing about growing old, you get fixed on one idea and you can't get it out of your head. Everything came out. It's like with aeroplanes, the black box. They fly along and everything's fine, the box says we've flown over the sea, over the mountains, gone through a storm, everything is just dandy; then the aeroplane crashes, they find the box and discover a couple of bolts that had been working loose for some time, add to that a slight wing tremor, first the tremor in the wing and then in the whole engine and then the plane explodes with all its secrets written down there in its black heart.

What am I saying? I don't know anything about aeroplanes, or black boxes, I've only read something about it in the papers. 'You talk just to give your tongue some exercise,' my father used to say. True. But you know since I've had nobody around I've got into this habit of talking to myself. I go on hour after hour, a kind of background noise like the radio, I ask myself all manner of questions and answer them, in no particular order. Look at my geranium. What should I do so it gets its colour back? It's all yellow, every morning I get up and I think I'll tear it up today, throw it out. Then I don't and it's still there, getting more and more dull and faded.

Every time you come to see me I'm amazed. Why? I wonder, it's not because you feel sorry for me, is it? What else could it be though? I'm just a poor old woman getting more stupid by the day. It's no good you saying otherwise. I can work that much out for myself. I go into a room to get something and when I'm there I don't remember what I went there for. I wander round a bit then I come back. You know what I did the other day? I drained the water without even putting the pasta in . . . It happens to you too? Maybe, but when you are young it's different, you forget because you've got other things on your mind. I'll tell you how I realized I was getting old. Before, your memories are stacked up in a neat pile, your good and bad memories, big and small ones. You know who you saw the day before and what happened on the last day of the year six years ago, everything's there in place like pearls on a string. Then all of a sudden you realize it's not like that any more, something has given way. It's a feeling as if memory is like the floor of a house, a wooden house, bit by bit some of the floorboards go rotten, even if they are crumbly they look the same as all the others, so you feel safe and you go on but then all of a sudden something vanishes, it disappears to another level you can't get at any more, the crossbeam gives way and everything around it, things disappear into the hole as if sucked in. The more the years go by the bigger the abyss gets, the whirlpools are eddying ever closer round you, you step more and more cautiously between the chasms, the slightest slip and even the little that you still have will finish up down there.

So it's all darkness, you see? It's dark but you are still alive, that's the worst thing of all, what makes you so angry. Your heart and your stomach keep going, they can go on year after year even when you're not there any more.

People round you look after you, give you choice tidbits to eat. When you dirty yourself they clean you like a child, they talk to you like a child too; they do everything they can for your heart, your stomach, they pretend the most important thing in the world is to keep those organs working. Now and then I think, the one stroke of luck I've had in my whole life is that I'm old and alone in the world and nobody will take the trouble to make sure my guts are still operational. Do you remember Mrs G.? Did you know her? Just think that for three months now her children have had to lock her in the house. Every morning she gets up, goes into the kitchen, she asks, where's my lunch-box? Then she says goodbye to everyone and says, 'Bye bye, I'm off to school ...' Do you see? It's much better if the firemen find you lying on the floor. Now and again when I'm sitting here in my armchair the whole afternoon, I see the light gradually fade away, the room is engulfed in shadows and I'm here, under my lamp reading something, my favourite poets,

I read a bit and then I put the book down because I get tired and with my eyes closed I think yes, of course we have a soul.

But then Mrs G. phones me, she says, 'I'm so happy, I got full marks for my maths, are you coming to my house to do your homework?' and I wonder to myself, if it exists, where has Mrs G.'s soul gone? Has it already flown up to wait for her body to join it? Or perhaps it doesn't exist and has never existed, there's nothing but heart, intestine, tongue. If it starts where does it start? If it ends where does it end? Where does it carry on after our death? Is there a warehouse for souls somewhere? Does it go from one body to the next like a dog looking for a master? These are things it's better not to ask, aren't they? Better just to accept than to start scratching the surface. But it's a bad habit I've always had, I can't get rid of it. I'm a hypocrite. What I should say is: there is no soul and that's fine. Instead of which I say, 'I would like for there to be one, perhaps there is and I just can't see it, I don't understand how it moves around. Does it peel away, does it stick and unstick itself? Maybe it's like a little ball and rolls along?'

When I was small my father was a strong believer in the Sabbath, he wanted us to respect it. So from sunset on Friday to sunset on Saturday we stopped doing anything. I really liked it, it was a bit like that game, I don't know if they still play it, statues, you walk and walk then when somebody gives the order you stop still. Saturday mornings my father and I would go for a walk around the city, just the two of us. Holding me tightly by the hand he would say to me, 'Look, you see, everything is double. You know why? Because today, and only today, you see with two sets of eyes, with your own eyes and with those of the soul.' It was a kind of magic, a spell. Children adore that sort of thing, it would be good if we could still enjoy them when we grew up. Yet it was more than just a notion, it was true. On Saturdays I heard noises, rustlings, whispers that I never heard on Sundays or Wednesdays. I saw everything double. On the one hand there was my body which was still, on the other hand something other which kept moving, darting between objects as nimbly as a fish, like a swift, agile eel. It's strange, but on those days I felt lighter, as if I were weightless. Did you have that feeling, too, when you were in Israel? You know what I mean then, you know what I'm talking about. Now and again I have this fantasy, that I'm an important politician, a head of state or something like that. You know what I would do if I were? Forget new laws, revolutions, no, I would simply impose one day of rest for everybody, not holidays, we already have those, but a day of proper rest. I'm convinced that everybody would be much the better for it. On Saturdays even my mother was at peace. She sat in an armchair near the gramophone and there she stayed the whole time. She waved her hands around gently, or else she hummed children's songs to herself. No matter how hard I think back I can never remember her having one of her violent crises on a Saturday. On other days she had them, yes. She had them worse than ever as the seasons changed over, between winter and spring or between summer and autumn. Her obsession was that she had viruses in her brain, they were there inside making it creak, slowly nibbling away at it. Her only salvation came from bees, they were the only ones who with their long stingers could pull them out one by one, they would make little boreholes, they would perforate her hair, the skin underneath, the dome of her skull, it would be a bloody, pitiless hunting down, but in the end the good insects would win and she would be safe for ever. That's how I remember her, in fact, standing at the window, her hair loose, calling down the swarms at the top of her voice. No, of course she wasn't born mad or my father would never have married her. Indeed if my grandparents were to be believed she was as sweet and willing a girl as you could find anywhere. It was my fault, it all began because of me, when I was born. What happened – they told me this when I was already grown up – was that two hours after giving birth she felt dirty, she wanted to wash and wash herself and when she saw me she shouted 'Take that disgusting thing away!'

Later the doctors said it would have happened anyway, something would have set it off, but what difference did that make to me? Meantime there I was, I was born and I was the daughter of a madwoman. A kind of stigma, do you see? Something which led me to live a little less. I was always aware of it, lying in wait for me. Have you ever been frightened of going mad too? I think that sooner or later it happens to everybody, it's normal in this life. But for me it was a bit more than that. I knew, indeed I know, that I have her blood in my veins and whatever it is whirling round inside me, sometimes at night I even seem to hear it, it goes round and round my veins and speaks to me, it says come on, come over here to me. Last week I saw a programme on the television about Japanese trees, those dwarf ones. How horrible, only the Japanese could dream up something like that! Do you know how they do it? They are trees like any other, all sorts, apple-trees, conifers, olive-trees. The seeds are the same, they have the same shape, the same leaves, the same colour, everything; they could, I mean they should grow but they can't because there's something keeping an eye on them, with a snip here and a snip there it squashes and compresses them, forces them to stay small. The same with me, when I was small I always made myself think very small, mediocre thoughts. I can very well remember, for example, that when I was an adolescent, when you naturally start thinking big thoughts, during the summer I would sometimes come home late in the evening, I walked along the sea shore and felt the starry sky above me, there it was over my head with all its stars like a big sheet, something which wraps you round, I knew it was there and I knew it was beautiful, very beautiful but I didn't raise my eyes, I didn't let myself. I was afraid, you understand? Afraid of the dark, the silence, the far off lights, afraid of that thing lying in wait for me. For years I would go on the beach without setting foot in the water, I never read a book unless somebody told me what it was about first.

My husband? I met him when I was still in my teens, after I met him things were a bit better. At that time my mother had been sent to a clinic. I didn't go to see her very often. It is the urge to live – you think about the future. He had just graduated in law, his pastime – I think you say hobby these days – was sculpture, just the right man for me in other words, calm and strong. I was thinking about marriage, children, my role as mother. It was during those very months that the first signs appeared.

I remember very clearly one March afternoon. It's strange this thing about the memory, isn't it? I don't know anything about what happened yesterday, but things from a long time ago are there before my eyes as if they'd happened just this minute. My father and I are in the sitting-room with the windows open, he's tuning his violin and I am reading. At one point a procession is passing by outside and shouting loudly in German – *Juden raus!* So I put down my book and ask my father, 'What are they saying?' Without putting down the violin he replies, 'They are saying *Jugend raus*, out with youth.' 'Why?' I ask. 'Because it's right,' says he. 'They're right, youth should go out, have a good time.'

You see? He refused to understand what was happening. It was a sin to betray your trust in God, I think that was part of it too.

Many years later, when it was all over, I thought, 'God's got nothing to do with it, perhaps he doesn't even exist. If he does exist he's busy somewhere else. It's not him who breathes viruses into your head or knocks them off balance, but his counterpart.'

I had a hard time coming to terms with it, though.

You know why? Partly because of his influence, partly because I was convinced that having a crazy mother would let me off anything else bad. We all have to pay our dues to suffering and I had already paid them, I was all right, nothing else could happen to me. So I concentrated on my trousseau, the engagement party, I waited for my future husband to call. That's how I lived, like so many other girls at that time. In the foreground were the two of us with our plans, history was far off in the background. How could I have imagined that she would be the one to drag us into it?

You know, now and again I happen to talk to young people like you and then I understand that you are much better than we were. You read, you find out about things, you look around you with eyes that don't miss a thing. I'm pleased about that, I think good, it won't happen again then. In our time it was very different: there were the big things like God, your soul, religion, and then there were the little everyday things. What was missing was – how can I put it? – the things in the middle.

When my mother was taken to hospital some strange pieces of news had already started to come out of Germany, news which nobody could credit. And in fact my father didn't believe what he heard. Even when some of his friends left for Palestine he stubbornly refused to take it all seriously. You know what he used to say? He said, 'People make such a fuss over nothing! We've never hurt anybody, why should anything happen to us?' He talked that way and of course I tried to go along with his way of thinking.

Funny, isn't it? Now as I look back over the whole

thing I realize that it's thanks to my mother that we got to safety. Perhaps I understood that yesterday and without realizing it that's why I burst out crying. Yesterday my heart understood, today it's my head. That's the way these things work, at a snail's pace. As I told you she'd already been in hospital three years when it happened. She'd got worse, it was no longer possible to keep her at home. In the clinic, though, she'd suddenly become very docile, she spent most of her time in bed practising a series of long and short whistles, a language she'd invented herself, she would call to her friends, the bees. Sometimes she would wave her arms in the air, as if to encourage them. That's the clearest image I have of her.

They took her away one morning in May; we knew nothing about it. I came to visit her with flowers in my hand, she always wanted flowers for her bees, and I found her bed empty and unmade. She wasn't in the bathroom, she wasn't in the corridor, I asked the doctors in a voice that was steadily rising 'Where is she?' And they stared at me without a word. In the courtyard I had passed a German lorry, all battened down with a soldier at the wheel. I'd seen it but I hadn't paid it any attention. It was only afterwards, as I paced up and down the corridors seeing those beds empty all of a sudden, that I suspected, or rather I knew for certain, and I ran outside, when I reached the courtyard the lorry's engines were starting up, it began to move off. I followed it, screaming, flowers were falling all around me, I can still see those flowers on the road, it didn't make any difference. Over the next few days we looked for her everywhere, my father pulled all the strings he could, there wasn't even a scrap of news. Disappeared, vanished for ever. The eugenics programme. You've heard of that, haven't you? Before even the Jews they eliminated the mentally handicapped, the mad. In the following weeks somebody let us know indirectly that she'd finished up in Germany, she'd finished up there for the purposes of scientific progress, to be part of some experiment. And someone else told as that she'd been finished off before she even got out of the city with the lorry's own exhaust pipe. I'm ashamed to tell you this but I still don't know where she is, where her body is, what's left of her. After the war they published detailed lists, I could have got hold of one and gone through all the names, but I didn't.

What if you did it? The lists are still available so you can tell me before I die. Me, no, for goodness sake, I wouldn't even dream of it. Grant me this one small luxury, not to see just this once, to be a coward.

That time, you know, the pain didn't make it in time, it froze solid like in a photograph. Suddenly that thing had happened to us, we had realized that it was all true. Above all else we had to think of ourselves, you see, of saving ourselves. My mother, the way she died, stayed down there inside, a little block of cement on the seabed. I knew my mother was dead, I knew I didn't know where she had died but I knew it like a statistic, a piece of news, not with my heart. Then yesterday with that interview something broke and came rushing out, not from my mouth but from my heart. I told you I hardly slept at all last night. I could feel my mother's body beside me, her little body like a bird's. I could hear her voice singing the song of the bees. You know what hurts more than anything else? Not being able to hold her hand in the last few minutes. I close my eyes and I can see her with her nightdress on, shoved into that lorry, tossed to the floor like a parcel, I think of her vacant, innocent look and then ... That's enough now, that's more than enough, I don't want to cry any more, not with you here. But you see, if she hadn't finished up like that we would have gone on for a long time not believing in the extermination and then it would have been too late. That's why I'm telling you she saved us. We all had the feeling that she was just there to be a burden, to make our lives difficult but then perhaps she was brought into the world and had lived with all that weight of suffering just for this, to allow us to go on living.

Is there a reckoning somewhere? With debits, credits, a settling of accounts? It's like with the soul, sometimes I think yes, sometimes no. I think of my mother, the point of her sacrifice and I think yes, but then I think what kind of reckoning is it that causes an innocent person to die? Nobody chooses, nobody decides, there is no reckoning, nothing. Things go on and that's that.

Now that really is enough, I'm starting to talk rubbish, things I don't know anything about. I've depressed you, haven't I? I don't know what's come over me, I've never talked so much, especially like this. It must be the sleepless night, I think, words are running away from me and I can't stop them.

Let's talk about you, or rather you talk, tell me something nice. What are you doing this evening when you leave here? Are you going dancing?

Look at those red cheeks! It's really windy today, isn't it? Are you sure you're dressed warmly enough? Don't laugh, that's the way I am, I never stop mothering people, you know what they say about Jewish mothers. Awful, they are. Please, would you go into the kitchen and make the tea, the pot is ready and waiting on the stove. I'll wait for you in the sitting-room, it's warmer there.

How it howls, even I can hear it though I'm so deaf. It's stupid but the wind always makes me strangely cheerful, like a child. It must be because it makes me think it passes through your head and blows all your troubles away. On days like this when my husband and I were engaged we always used to go up that mountain there, the Carso.

On the edge of the plateau there's a little saddle, I don't know if you know it, if you've ever been there. There the wind blows stronger than anywhere else, it gathers itself up before exploding over the city. We spent hour after hour there and at each strong gust we would let ourselves lean into the wind, the trick was not to fall when it suddenly quietened down again. Just this morning while I was still in bed listening to everything rattling those afternoons came back to me and do you know what suddenly happened to me? I wanted to go back up there. I haven't been back there since we were engaged. You can understand why, you know me by now, I never want to remember anything. But this morning I surprised myself, I thought yes, I want to go up there, I want to see the saddle covered in grass, I want to feel the icy wind in my face, on my nose, in my ears. For one last time I want to see it all.

Why do I say last? Because that's the way it is, I can feel it. It must have happened to you too, no? You go on a journey, you're in a lovely place but then you have to leave. So what do you do? You go to your favourite spot and you stop and look at it. It's one way of keeping things inside, you put them in a kind of secret suitcase. In the same way you get to an age when you suddenly want to do the same, I've felt that way for a couple of months now. Of course I don't move an inch, I don't go anywhere, my health won't let me nor my finances, but yes, I would like to go back to those places, say goodbye one last time to all those things which watched me living. There's that poem, who's it by? Rilke if I'm not mistaken or perhaps I'm wrong. Anyway there's a poem which expresses that feeling perfectly. I remember a bit in German, just a couple of lines, what are they now? No, I can't get them out, I can't do it any more. To think I used to like it so much, more than a simple pleasure it was my first language, even now I don't think there's a better one for poetry.

Bruno, you know, my husband, was in the habit of learning his favourite ones off by heart. He used to say they are like tender music for the soul, you should always have them ready for you inside. He taught me the few verses I know, I had a bad memory even when I was young. When he came back he said, it's thanks to them I'm still alive, that I managed to save myself. He used to say them over and over during the worst moments, you see? When he was supposed to be nothing more than an animal he used to say them to himself, inside his head, they were a treasure nobody could take away from him.

How did it happen? We were hiding in a flat, we were already married and there we were, my father had managed to get on a boat for Palestine, we were to leave on the next ship. Some of my father's friends had let us use that flat, it was on the top floor of a block near the station. We lived hidden away, of course, with the windows and curtains always shut. We waited for the people downstairs to move before we did. We'd become expert at it, we spoke under our breath, we walked round in the dark with no shoes on. Before pulling the flush we waited for them to pull theirs, the noises had to be identical so they would merge in together, they had to be an exact match. We stayed there three months, it was our honeymoon. Then one morning when every-thing seemed quiet he decided to go out, to go and find out about the ship. I stood at the window, the shutters were wooden and a bit dilapidated. I could see every-thing perfectly clearly, I saw him go out with his hat on, cross the square. Half-way across a car came up to him, a man got out, they exchanged a few brief words then the man grabbed him by the arm and bundled him inside the car. He didn't turn round to look at me, he didn't want to give me away you see, but I could see his eyes, the expression on his face, just the same. I still don't know how long I stood there, like a hunted beast. I'd heard the bloodhounds all around. I was waiting for them, I don't remember what I thought those long hours, it wasn't me there. All of a sudden my body, my head had been transformed. I'd become like one of those animals that sleep under the ice. What are they called? Marmots? Yes, that's it, I'd turned into a marmot. Then darkness fell, I stirred, I thought what do I do? All I could think was, they've got him, soon, very soon, they'll come and get me too. I was in a corner of the room, and with my face to the wall I fell to my knees and very quietly, without making any noise, I cried for hour after hour. That morning I'd said goodbye to him same as ever, a bit hastily even. I'd said goodbye to him in that way because I didn't know, I didn't even dream that he would disappear. So I had that feeling of remorse that I hadn't hugged him tighter, that I hadn't looked long into his eyes. It's daft really, isn't it? We'd known each other so many years, how could I forget him, forget his voice, his body? But the fact that I hadn't been able to say goodbye properly, knowing it was the last time, made me cry. I was afraid I would soon forget him, that I would mix him up with other people.

Was I afraid for myself? No, I didn't care about myself. All I wanted was for it all to be over as fast as possible. No, the thought of death didn't frighten me, on the contrary. As you know I went to that convent, it was the underground organization who arranged everything. I left on the last night of Carnival, we'd deliberately waited until then to take advantage of the general hubbub. Hidden in the back of a van I was taken to a convent near the mountains. I stayed there until the end of the war. Two months later I got news about Bruno. They hadn't killed him, he was still in Italy in a transit camp, nobody knew when he would be leaving.

Then I found some strength, the strength I thought I didn't have any more. I could only think of freeing him, of getting him out as fast as possible, before he left for Germany. It was exhausting though. Every day I got disheartened, I was frightened I wouldn't make it. Day after day, week after empty week went by. There was a little fountain with a madonna on top and goldfish in it. I would look at those goldfish and they would look at me, I would think of the last piece of news I'd had and the other piece of news which never came. And then, you know how it happens don't you? It must have happened to you on a journey or when you've been ill. You think and think, you can't talk to anyone and so after a while you no longer know what's true and what isn't, you become unsure about everything. I started to suspect they were having me on, that out of pity they were saying things that weren't true. But then one day, what month was it? May, I think, on the altar there was a big bunch of poppies and cornflowers, yes, one morning in May, it was a secret signal, it was the news I'd been waiting for. The plan by now was ready down to the finest detail, before the end of the month Bruno would be able to escape.

Do you know what I did that day? I went by myself

to the chapel and on my knees, like a child, I said, 'Thank you God!'

But what do I know, what do I understand, who am I thanking? Never a stable point, a law which always holds, each time I invent one it is proved wrong. I say this is God's law, it's fate, it's a sense of guilt, it's redemption: I expect something to happen and the opposite happens, a bit as if a new law were always in operation, a law you don't expect. It's the same with evil: I thought I had paid for my sin. But it wasn't finished. Each time you turn round you are hit in the face. That's what life is like, you know; we are like worms turned up by the spade, the light suddenly catches us, we thrash about like mad things, birds are attracted by all the wriggling, they hurl themselves on us, some of us get eaten and others not, we thrash about some more and then the spade throws more earth over us, covers us over and once more we are in the dark silence, we are still. Perhaps you think I'm too much of a pessimist? Hope, you say? What am I to do with that? I've looked at life with my own eyes, I've followed it from beginning to end and now that I'm old and look back I know what it's all about.

To come to the point: it seems unbelievable, but Bruno didn't want to escape, he refused. He could have, the plan was ready, perfect, the risks were minimal. He could have, but he didn't. He said thank you, no, I'm staying here. I never knew why, even when he came back I never had the courage to ask him. I've wondered about it so often, and do you know what I think? His reaction was part of his character, he was a man of integrity, loyal, his life was there in the struggle against injustice. Perhaps, too, he didn't want any privilege, to live while all the others were going off to die. He trusted in destiny, more than trust, even: he had faith. If destiny was holding out death to him, even the most appalling death, he would accept it without a murmur. I still don't know what to call it. Courage? Cowardice? You know what I'm like, one day I think one thing, the next something else. But you'll agree with me there, won't you? Following your destiny is easier, you never have to ask yourself anything, you never have to make a choice.

But all this, you see, all this was a great big thing which went right over my head. How else could you expect me to feel? I had a husband, a husband I loved and when it came down to a choice between destiny and me, he chose destiny. Where did that leave me? I was no more than an accessory.

It's wicked of me to talk this way, isn't it? But I can't deny it, I was bitterly disappointed, I felt betrayed. Time didn't exist for me any more, everything had come to a halt, the days in the convent went by one the same as the next. It was impossible to believe he would come back; life had taken that particular turn and would follow its course right to the end. Something would happen, for sure; one day the war would be over and I would be free again, but what did I care about that? I'd spent a whole year on my trousseau. I'd embroidered all the sheets, the pillowcases, the tablecloths, and they were still there in my father's cellar in cardboard boxes, tied up tight with string.

From my cell window I could see nothing but fields,

they were planted with wheat. In the summer after-noons, between two and three, that terrible time when you don't know what to do with yourself, I used to stand there and look out. Beauty can be a terrible thing, can't it? It can be more frightening than anything else, more horrific. The fields were still, absolutely still, sure of themselves, there wasn't a breath of wind, one long wave of solid gold that went on and on as far as the eye could see. Why am I telling you this? Because of the cicadas, that's why. Because of the noise they make, the whirring sound. Swallows chatter and cicadas whirr, that's right. I could hear the din they made and every quarter of an hour the convent bells. I heard them striking slowly, one after the other, and the buzzing of the occasional fly. Insects would flutter round my face to suck up the drops of sweat and then, then ... How did I come to be saying all this? I've forgotten what I was saying ... Oh yes, nature.

You see, it's very fashionable nowadays to rescue every living ant. Every morning I open the paper and read that a species of tree is disappearing, there are hardly any frogs left, there's a hole up there in the sky, an enormous hole. I read all about these things and I don't understand, I can't see how you can get so attached to them, love them even. You're fond of nature, aren't you? You told me that once, I don't know why you like it, for me nature is nothing but an insult, a slap in the face.

Where did we get to? The convent? Yes, I spent three whole years living with the nuns. We didn't have much to say to each other, but they were kind; besides, they were running a huge risk keeping me there. I helped out in the kitchen, in the orchard, I fed the chickens, I didn't want to be a burden on them. After a while that kind of life has a strange effect on you, it acts like a kind of anaesthetic.

So almost without realizing it, at a certain point I made an oath – no, what's the word? a vow – I made a vow to God, the first and last in my whole life, I promised him that at the end of the war I would stay within those walls, I would spend the rest of my life closed in there in all humility, away from the eyes of other people. I wanted to atone, I thought then. Now I think that was just another piece of cowardice. I wanted to crawl into a hole, that's all.

Luckily the sisters knew nothing about it, it was a deal between me and him, private, so at least I didn't have to hang my head in shame before them when I broke my word.

You know what I thought when I got home? I thought well, deep down I haven't broken any vow because I made it with the Christian God, while my God is another. You see? As if God presided over just the one club. I was frightened he would take his revenge, certainly, you know how angry the God of the Bible gets. But that fear didn't last long. There was my life to begin all over, everything had to be put back together again. Bruno came back with the last convoy of survivors.

Why don't you ever tell me anything about your boyfriends? You don't have any? I don't believe you. How could I? You're pretty, you have a heart, don't you? Or maybe not? Sometimes you come here and while we are talking I look at you and I am a little afraid of you. No, not afraid, you make me uneasy. I can never work out what lies behind your smile, behind your eyes. Now and then I say, she has a big heart, she's a lovely girl, other times I see a glint in your eyes and I think the opposite. But then why ask, what does it matter? You come here and you listen to me.

You've brought some sewing with you today? I'm sorry, but it makes me laugh to see you like that, with needle and thread in hand, I didn't know you knew how. You're learning? Good for you, I never managed it, I never learnt to do a thing in my life, just cook a bit, the plainest of dishes. My mother was crazy, my father thought I would have servants. So when I was of an age nobody ever taught me a thing. You teach yourself? Maybe. Yes, if you want to you can do anything, but I never had a great deal of initiative. I think the way I was brought up is to blame, I often look at my friends' grandchildren, I listen to them talking to each other and their parents and I think goodness, they have no idea how easy their lives are. When I was a young girl we were encouraged to be obedient, I'm not saying we were frightened, not in my case anyway, but we showed respect. We had a lot of respect for our parents, for our parents and then later for our husbands. It was all part of the same pattern, we loved them and they loved us, but we never dared to disagree.

In any case with Bruno I was very lucky. He was very open-minded for those days, he let me decide things freely for myself, at least in theory he let me because in reality I never decided a thing.

It was hard when he came back, you know. I'd spent three years convincing myself I would never see him again. If truth be told, I shouldn't have convinced myself of that, I should never have given up hope, but that's just the way I am. I'd convinced myself he was dead, instead of which one day I suddenly had him there at home again. We had to begin our lives as husband and wife, the life we had never led together. He was twenty-six years old, I was only twenty-two, twenty-two, do you hear? To tell the truth I don't know how old we were, we felt so old and so tired ... Now and then in the evening, when we were at home, I watched him as he lay asleep in the armchair with the radio on and I was overcome by a sense of unreality. I think the same happened to him, too.

I never asked him any questions, it didn't seem right. I listened to him when he talked, but that was rare. He was the shadow, the ghost of the man I'd married. Yes, maybe I was different too, those three years of solitude had done something to me inside. I don't know how I'd changed though, when you are always alone with yourself it's hard to notice the difference.

Anyway, if Bruno was peaceful during the day, at night he was always restless, night-time was real hell. I often had to patch up the sheets in the morning because they were torn. It was Bruno who tore them. He tossed about as if an electric current were passing through him, his arms and legs flailed about and he would grind his teeth. I never knew what to do, I never knew whether to wake him up or not. I would sit on the edge of the bed and watch him, I would listen to what he was saying, trying to understand what was happening. He always shouted in German, he shouted orders. That's why, I've already told you haven't I? I can't speak German any more. After the war, especially in recent years, a lot of books have come out, books by survivors, by psychologists, by historians. I've seen them on the bookshop shelves, I've never picked them up to have a look.

I don't want to know, I'm not interested, for me it's all there in those night cries, in the ripped sheets.

A strange thing happened the other day in the street, something which has never happened to me before. I'd gone to the nearby row of shops to buy some milk. I was making my way back home as fast as my arthritic old legs would carry me. It's the arthritis, you know, that makes me walk along with my head hanging down. I was half-way along when I realized that there were plants, ugly city plants, growing out of the pavement. They were sticking out of the tiny cracks, growing up tough and strong.

I don't know what happened. I suddenly found myself on my knees. There I was, on the ground, tugging at them, I was tearing them out one by one and shouting, 'Away with you, get out, damn you!' Only when a man came and lifted me by the arm, when I was on my feet again, did I understand where I was and what I was doing. At the time, naturally, I was so ashamed I wished the ground would swallow me up, I moved away as fast as I could, sneaking off like a thief.

That incident stayed with me all afternoon and all night. What did I have to tear out those plants for, they might have been ugly but they had never done me any harm. What was going on in my head? I came to the conclusion that it was their desperate tenacity that got on my nerves. Life is tough, a bully. It wants to keep on moving and that's exactly what it does, it doesn't give a damn about anything else, it will trample all over your feelings.

It's a natural law, you say? To protect the genetic patrimony, to propagate it? Exactly, and what does that mean? A slap in the face, like I said.

It was the same with me and Bruno. We should have split up, disappeared into thin air, perhaps to crop up again somewhere else like the Indians say and have a calm, decent life. But no, there we were, tired, we didn't know what to say to each other, we only had just enough strength to get us through to evening. But something stopped us calling it a day. Even though we didn't want to, something made us carry on, drag on. As soon as his health was restored, Bruno started thinking about work. Within a couple of months he'd found a lawyer's practice willing to take him on as partner, and so our life soon turned into the ordinary, quiet life of every young bourgeois couple. But it wasn't true, do you understand? Over our heads, inside us, we still had those three terrible years. Certainly they had been worse for him than for me. Now and then at dinner I watched him eat. He ate fast, like an animal, his eyes fixed on his plate. More than eat, he devoured his food, as if he was afraid it would be the last time, or as if he thought a wilder beast was going to take it away from him. His way of doing things soon got to me, too. We weren't sure about anything any more.

I'm not saying he'd changed, no. He was still the strong man of integrity I'd always known, but sometimes he just went off his head. If he came home and the dinner wasn't ready he would yell like a madman, he'd smash everything. I didn't know how to cope with it. I wanted to help him and be close to him but I was scared. After those scenes he would suddenly go quiet, he'd sit there in his armchair staring into space or he'd go out; he disappeared for hours on end. I think he was ashamed of himself, it wasn't like him to behave like that. After those scenes I often found myself alone in the house and wondering why I didn't get caught too, why we didn't die together? Why him and not me, why had fate decided that way and what did it hold in store for me?

Naturally I hoped that in time everything would sort itself out. I thought to myself that if his body had got its strength back, his mind would soon recover too. Time's a great healer, it dulls the sharpest pain.

If they try to tell you that, don't believe a word of it, it's not true. It's something people say to make themselves feel better and that's all. Occasionally time seems to heal, but it's only a false impression, completely false. Time works away underneath, it's like a little drill, it digs away, down, it turns holes into a chasm, an abyss.

It's very strange that some things you only understand as you get old. We would have a better life if we understood them earlier, instead of which we only understand when it's all over and it's too late to be of any use, all you can do with your new-found knowledge is chatter on like I do with you. If old people talked more to young people and if young people listened, perhaps something would change . . . or perhaps not, it wouldn't be any use. Every life is a tragedy right from the beginning. Talking about it is wasted breath, everybody makes mistakes and then when we are old we understand, we regret our mistakes. Experience counts for nothing, everybody has to start from the beginning.

You think it would be monotonous any other way? Maybe so, but who ever said monotony was a bad thing? Experience makes you grow? I don't believe that because the world is still the same, you still see the same dramas being played out. You know what I would have liked? I would like to have been a tree, a cypress, a sacred olive, a plant with roots underground and branches waving in the air. Plants can feel too? They've discovered that in America?! No, I didn't know that, in that case I take it all back, I don't want to be like a tree, forget it.

But there you are, at twenty-four I had no idea about all this. Bruno's work was going quite well now, I saw to the house; in spring we were both swept up in a kind of euphoria, a euphoria we hadn't felt since we were engaged, we felt a kind of drive in us, and having a child seemed the most natural thing in the world. It was life taking hold again, you see?

Indeed, when I realized that I was in an interesting condition I thought that we'd finally be able to draw a line under what had happened. With that child it was as if we could say that's enough, full stop, everything will be different now. The first months I was happy, we were happy. You wouldn't know but when a woman falls pregnant something happens in her body, a kind of obtuseness spreads through her. Every day something is different, you look at yourself in the mirror and you see your eyes are beautiful, shining. There are some inconveniences, certainly, but you barely notice them, you are radiant, radiant inside because you feel that there is an order, and you are part of that order. For me there was even more to it than that; I hoped that having a baby around would help Bruno to get better, to stop looking over his shoulder. Other people we knew who were in a similar position had got out of it by having a child. Why should things be any different for us?

As autumn came on Bruno became very sullen and had several really bad patches. During one of his crises he disappeared from the house for two whole days. He had those bad spells but I still carried on hoping, I said to myself when you think about it, the child is still inside, Bruno can't see him yet. When he can see him with his own eyes, things will be better.

I gave birth in December, all perfectly straight-forward. The next day we were still in the clinic and Bruno took a photograph of me holding the baby. It was for my father, I wanted him to know that life went on and that I had found the strength to carry on. Come the end of the war he'd stayed over there, he'd got married again. He lived in a kibbutz, he sounded happy in his letters.

It may seem odd but I don't remember much about

the first few months. The new baby girl took up all my time and energy. Not that she was a difficult baby, no, she was perfectly normal. What destroys you is that they can't get through a single hour without you, without you doing something for them. During the week Bruno was always at the office, he didn't even come home for lunch. Saturday was the only day we spent together. If it was a nice day we went for a walk along the beach. We didn't talk much those months, we never talked much, but I was aware of something between us that was strong, solid, something I had never felt before. I think it was pride, happiness, determination. I felt that we'd been right to go ahead, that we were winning. You only had to look at the baby to see that, she was brighter and gurgled more every day. She didn't seem to have suffered from anything that had gone before. Bruno was besotted with her, he would pick her up as soon as he could. It was unusual in those days you know, fathers never spent time with their small children, they left everything to the women, they were afraid of hurting the child or of getting dirty. Usually they began to remember they had a child when they started going to school. Bruno was different though, he fell in love with his daughter straight away and spent all his spare time with her.

You can imagine how I felt, can't you? For the first time since I could remember there were no clouds on my horizon, the sky was a bright, clear blue.

I could see the whole future laid out in front of me, Serena growing up, the passing of the years. Her growing up and us getting old, we would grow old under that clear sky and then one day like a candle that burns down bit by bit, under that same sky we would go out. Now and then, to bolster myself up – there was still a corner of me that wasn't so sure – I even made mental calculations. I cast my mind over all the people I knew and I said So and so has already had this and this to deal with, nothing else will happen to him, but What's his name has had a marvellous life up to now so perhaps he should be on the lookout for something. There I was like a chemist, weighing everything up and in the end I came to my own conclusions. It was always the same conclusion: if you suffer before, you don't suffer afterwards as well. It was a childish game, childish and pig-headed but it helped to keep me calm. I wanted to be sure that our lives were safe. The relationship we have to suffering is a strange one, you know. While our suffering is still small we rebel, we think that if one terrible thing has happened, there will be no others . . . Why? Because it's not fair. It's as if we have inside us an infallible sense of fair play. We think life is a holiday and suffering is like a slice of cake – one each and that's our lot.

But then, I don't know if it's a question of biology, too, you get old, you aren't as strong. Then one day you wake up and you don't expect anything else, you expect nothing but bad things. You start to think differently, you're there all the time lying beneath the sun like some animal with its back broken. Even if you want to move you can't, you stay there and you wait.

Have you ever thought of having a child? I've heard it's the thing nowadays for women to have them on their own, without a father I mean. Yes, maybe when they're smaller it's easier; but when they grow up what are you going to tell them?

Would you do it like that? I didn't think you were so sensible. You say a baby is an act of love? That's right in theory, certainly, but believe me that no one who's been a parent would ever say that. Do you want to know what a child is? It's a container you throw everything into, you throw in all the things you haven't got but which you'd like to have. With a child, you see, every time you move a finger you get it wrong. Can we save ourselves by recognizing our errors? No, it's not like that. I've always recognized them, right from the start but it never did any good. Because you're so busy throwing in this, that and the other you forget the container already exists, that it already has its own story.

Do you know that game of straws? There are lots of you, you have to do something but since nobody wants to do it you decide with straws. There are short ones and long ones, the person who pulls the shortest one has to do it even if he doesn't want to. So even if you won't acknowledge it, even if you fool yourself that you are shaping him, in reality your child, your child and all the children who come into the world, have their straw in their hand and everything is written on that piece of straw, it's a game of chance which goes on above you, before you, in spite of you.

Yes, you're right, we can choose, too. When you are thirty you might think you can choose, it's right that it should be that way; but not at eighty, no, you don't believe that any longer. With time you understand it's not like that, it's the difference between active and passive, rather than choosing we are chosen.

What for? Who by? Don't ask me that. That's what I've thought, and it's what I still think; my life goes no further.

Give me your jacket, it's hot. Spring has arrived all of a sudden, no one was expecting it. Every time I see you walking up the corridor you look bigger to me. You're not still growing? Perhaps it's me getting smaller. That's what happens when you get old, your flesh dries up on your bones and your bones get thinner, it's as if everything is getting ready in silence to go away, to disappear ... Yet you look bigger than you did last week. Do you do a lot of exercise? Maybe that's why. No, you know what it is? It's because I envy you, not so much for me, I am what I am, but I would like to have had a daughter like you. Serena was always round shouldered, her face sunk in, she was terrible to look at, she looked as if she was expecting someone to hit her any moment. So I was always saying to her, 'Sit up, look straight ahead of you, can't you see you look like an old woman?!' She made me angry because I was like that at her age, too, I was like that and I've stayed that way. I wished she'd looked like Bruno, he had the body of an athlete, with broad shoulders; when he was young he did a lot of sport, when he came back from the camp you could still see he'd been a strong man. You see? It's the story of the container repeating itself. Your parents probably wanted a completely different baby, too, didn't they?

Did I say the baby was bright and happy? It's true, she was, from the day she was born until she was almost two years old. That's why I felt so betrayed, so deceived. She promised to be one thing, she turned out to be another.

That happy picture of the two of us with the baby didn't last for long. As soon as Serena started talking and getting round the house Bruno changed, everything started getting on his nerves. It's a very difficult age, two to three years, you have to be running after them all the time, mind they don't hurt themselves and don't fall. They want to try things, they pick things up and drop them on the ground and smash them. You need a lot of patience. Then they start playing up. A psychologist friend of mine told me they do it on purpose, it's a way of proving to themselves and to other people that they are there in the world. We didn't know that in those days, she was playing up and that was that, she had to be checked. So one day over dinner Bruno exploded – she'd thrown her spoon on the floor three times, she was refusing to eat. Completely out of the blue he got up and shouted, 'You don't know how lucky you are!' and he walked out of the house slamming the door.

It was next morning before he came back home. I didn't ask him where he'd been, I suspected he didn't know himself. But that day was a kind of declaration of war. He was always there with his eyes peeled to see if the baby did any damage. He would tell me off, say I didn't have a firm enough hand. Now and then he would rant and then disappear for days at a stretch. I tried to keep the baby under control, to keep her quiet; I could only do that so much, I think she was aware of the bad feeling because she got more and more awkward every day. You see, the whole meaning to my life was there in the two of them, and all of a sudden neither of them took the slightest notice of me. There was war between the two of them and I was in the middle like a stake between two fires. The reason? I'm not sure, but what I think is that deep down inside, in a place that even he wasn't aware of, Bruno had begun to hate life, and Serena was life. Yes, I tried to talk to him once after a particularly bad scene. When he came back home I carried on as normal but once Serena was in bed I sat down with him in the living-room, sat down opposite him and said, 'Bruno, I have to talk to you.' That's all I said, he suddenly burst into tears, he had his hands over his face and he was crying, his body racked by sobs, like a little boy.

The following month, after a couple of missed phone calls, I found out he often didn't show up at the office. To the people in the office he said he was working at home, at home he said he was going to the office. Where did he go? I never found out, I had the little girl, I couldn't go after him. When he was with us he got more and more withdrawn. Even on Saturdays, instead of coming with us to the seaside he would go off on his own. To try to work out something of what was happening do you know what I used to do? I would look him in the eyes. I could watch him at my leisure for hours because he was never aware of what was going on, he would stare emptily into the distance. One day I received a letter, you know, a letter like you see in the films, written with letters and words cut out from the papers. This letter said he had a lover, perhaps another family even, and that was why he was never at home with us. Did I believe it? Not for a moment, I opened it, read it, screwed it up and put a match to it. Do you see? I didn't want him to find it, to have to put up with people's nastiness as well. Because you see his nights were different now, they'd gone back to being like they were before, he would scream with his eyes shut and tear at his pyjamas. I wasn't certain – you can never be certain of anything – but I suspected that that was the reason for all his odd behaviour; the three years had come back, day by day they were gnawing away at his insides. Can you picture a river which carries sand and rubbish along with it? Very gradually, inch by inch, the sand and the rubbish make the sea disappear, they swallow it up. Something of the kind was happening inside his head.

Just once, in those years, I came across him in the street. It was completely by chance, it was a nice day and I had taken Serena to the port to see the ships. No, he didn't see us. I don't think Serena realized her father was nearby either. I was the only one to recognize him by an odd way he had of stuffing his hands in his pockets. What was he doing? Nothing, he was sitting at the end of the pier between two fishermen, he didn't seem to know them. They fished and he watched them fishing. When one of them reeled in a fish he didn't look up from the water, he carried on staring down.

Seeing him there, you know, even if he wasn't doing anything in particular, had really shaken me, something jolted inside. What? A cloud, the first big black cloud on the horizon which I was so determined should be blue. Then, I don't know if this has ever happened to you, but there are times when you still don't know anything and in reality you know everything. Perhaps they are paranormal powers?

No, that's hard to believe. Rather I think that in some part of you which you're not aware of you've already stored up clues, signals, like a kind of puzzle. When it happens, and only when it happens, you realize that that is what was missing, the last piece of the jigsaw.

So that afternoon when the phone went – it was autumn, it was raining, I remember, I'd just given Serena her tea – even before picking up the phone I knew what it was, I wasn't in the least surprised when I heard it was the police. Before they could say anything else I asked, 'Where is he?'

I was wrong only about the place. That's why you're wrong when you say it's foresight. I thought he'd let himself fall into the water, that he'd drowned. Actually his body was up the hill, cut into three pieces by a train.

No, I've never seen the place. Even years after I always tried to avoid it. Where is it? I think it's not far from that cattle depot where they collect the cows arriving in trucks from the east. Do you know it? Is it awful at night? Do the animals make a lot of noise? Do you think cows can feel anything too? No it's impossible, animals can't understand, they can't possibly know that they are going to die the next day. Anyway Bruno, so the police told me, had made a kind of shelter for himself around there, I think that's where he went when he disappeared for days on end. Inside they found his shoes, a folder with pieces cut out of the paper. No, I didn't think any more of it, I had Serena, I had to think of her, I was a mother you understand? There were a lot of practical matters to be sorted out and even though I'd told her Daddy had gone away, she must have guessed something. She was odd, every time I looked at her closely – when she was asleep or when she was doing her homework – I realized she was coming to look more and more like Bruno. It was as if part of his spirit had broken off and settled inside her, but it wasn't his good, strong part. It was the weak, lost part of recent years. At school she was doing fine, she was obviously an intelligent child. Perhaps that was her undoing, her intelligence. They say intelligence is a gift but I don't believe it. It would be much, much better to live without it. At school she was fine but she didn't have any friends, she was always on her own, she wasn't interested in anything. I would try and get her to go out or read books, you know the way mothers do. I was afraid she would close in on herself too much. Don't forget that behind her, inside her, there was my mother, too. I wasn't sure but it could be ...

Bruno and I had completely forgotten about the dangers of heredity, you see. What's the word they use nowadays, repressed? Well, we'd repressed it. It's nature, as I've already explained to you. To get its own way it really hits below the belt.

When I was left on my own with Serena it all came back to me. It became something of an obsession, perhaps I kept too close tabs on her, I watched her every movement. I wondered is that normal? isn't it normal?

She was always crying. She started crying much earlier than girls usually do, when they are teenagers. She was always bursting into tears for no reason at all. I would ask her, why are you crying? And she would cry even louder, shout 'I don't know!' and fling her arms round my neck. In those days there was none of this stuff about psychology or psychoanalysis. You went to the psychiatrist if you were mad, everything else was a matter of common sense, common sense and that was all. So I would comfort her, hold her in my arms, but sometimes I'd had enough, too, I left her there on her own, crying for hour after hour. I never let her see it but I was frightened too, I felt as though yet again things were slipping out of my grasp. Serena was the only thing I had left.

You know, the afternoons I'm here on my own sitting in my chair, I switch on the television, I flick through the channels, nothing ever appeals to me. But when I find a science programme, one of those programmes which explains how things work inside, I switch it off. It might be interesting but I want nothing to do with it. I can't stand all that stuff about genes and chromosomes. I can't stand seeing everything in coloured illustrations, enlargements of what you can see under the microscope: baby mouse does this because mummy mouse does that and all that sort of thing ... It's terrible, absolutely unbearable.

She was fifteen years old when she tried to take her own life. I found her on the sofa, she was stretched out there, still breathing.

While she was in hospital I realized you can never

escape, escape is an illusion. The years Bruno had spent in Germany were all there inside, stamped into his genes. Scientists might say otherwise, that it's not true, but I'm telling you that everything leaves a trace. It was as if she'd been there, suffered along with her father; perhaps she was suffering even more because she didn't know why she was suffering. It was something that was tearing her apart, she had no skin left to cover her, no protection, the slightest breeze made her jump. It was my fault for bringing her into the world.

In Israel they're studying the effects of extermination camps on younger generations, are they? So you see, I'm right, it's true. The horror gets into your very being, it's transmitted to your children and then your children's children ... it goes on from generation to generation, very gradually it fades until it disappears altogether. It disappears exactly at the time another horror lies in wait, fresh and alive it's there waiting and ... I've forgotten what I was talking about ... Can you hear that buzzing noise? What could it be? The fridge?

What were we talking about? I think ... Yes, that's it. I don't believe the story of the good Samaritan; if good people existed we would be able to spot them. I don't see them anywhere. I'm not good either, I can't fool myself to that extent, I'm good for nothing, there's nothing good because all this evil, this thing that swamps us and gets inside us and makes us do things an animal would never do ... animals only eat other animals destined to be eaten, they don't devour indiscriminately just for the sake of it ... Where does that urge come from? From men, from their hearts: who put it there? Did somebody put it there? We went to the mountains, we slept in the same room, in the same bed. It was the first time we'd done that since she was small. One night I woke up with screaming in my ears – I didn't know where I was, for a moment I thought it was Bruno – then I switched on the light and I realized it was her, my baby. She was screaming, her eyes were closed, her arms and legs were rigid. I sat on the edge of the bed. I sat still, not knowing what to do. At night, time goes by differently, it expands and dilates. Suddenly that deal came into my mind, the deal I'd made with God all those years before. There you are, I thought, I tried to cheat him, I'd asked for peace in exchange for something which I never gave... Now he was in the right, he was furious and he was punishing me. My life could be different, it's my own fault if at some stage it took the turn it did. It's turned itself inside out, shrivelled and curled up at the edges, it's gone crooked and twisted with suffering.

I could have got out of it all, couldn't I? I could have killed myself, called checkmate, it was the only freedom left to me and I didn't take it. I would be lying if I said I was thinking of Serena or something of the kind. She'd been there all along with her straw clutched tightly in her hand... I'd seen the straw, there was nothing I could do. It isn't because of her or because of anybody else that I'm not dead, I'm just a coward.

I drew back the curtains to let the daylight in. All those pine-trees outside and over it all a bird hanging in the air, it was almost still, perhaps it was a falcon, Serena switched on the radio, there was a song playing, I remember one line, it said 'his big mess of a life ...'

During the week I sit here in my chair and wait for you to arrive. I think I won't tell her anything, I'll talk about the weather, the little that I know about politics. I would like to sew up my mouth, inside me it's sewn up, I'm sure, but when I see you I don't know what happens, it opens up and starts off all by itself ... That song, do you see? There comes a point when the whole thing's ridiculous.

My best friend's granddaughter has died. She was barely a toddler, she'd just learned to talk. All of a sudden she couldn't see properly, a new form of life had sprung up inside her – cancer here, there, all over the place, tough, overpowering nature, it swallowed up her brain and everything else. I was close to her at the funeral, but I wanted to laugh out loud.

Innocence which suffers and dies, what is that? I'd like to ask all those people who get down on bended knee, can they answer me that?

It must have happened to you too, hasn't it? Faced with sadness, instead of crying you start laughing, you laugh and laugh and you can't stop. It's not right but you laugh anyway, evil makes you laugh. A little evil makes you cry, but a lot makes you laugh. You laugh like in the comics when not just one thing breaks but everything is smashed. Everything falls to pieces, even the hero, and we find it funny. That's how my life is, I tell you one thing after another, for a bit you believe it but there comes a point when something happens, you think it's all too much and you want to laugh. The reason why I've never told anybody – never told the whole story, I mean – is that inevitable laughter. You're not laughing yet, you don't look as if you're laughing, but how do I know what you're thinking inside? Perhaps you're just being polite.

I have this bad habit of looking at other people's lives. I look at them and I say, they're like fruit from the supermarket – you know, the fruit you get nowadays, all the same, round and all the same colour – I've seen it on the television, apparently they do it with hormones, that's what gives us cancer in the end or at least makes it more likely, but what do we care, in the meantime we have perfect fruit. I'm told they clone flowers, too, I don't know what that word means, it makes me think of something rude. Cloned roses are all roses to the hilt, they couldn't be more rose than that, there's just one thing missing, they have no scent any more.

Now and again my father used to write to me from over there. He worked on a farm, their methods were bang up to date, nobody produced as many calves as they did, calves like fruit, like in a children's schoolbook, all of them absolutely identical, impeccable. But then out of every hundred one would be born with two heads, with three legs. There'd be a revolt; it doesn't happen often but it happens. Two pears are formed stuck together, they have the stem, the flesh, seeds, but there are two of them – an error of nature – they go into the museums, into books, into the rubbish. So I look at other people's lives and I see that for the most part they are peaceful, only tiny little things happen to them, people live peacefully and then they die peacefully. You only have to look around, you can see for yourself, you can see normality flowing along or rushing by, but then every now and then there's a slip-up. I don't know quite when it happens, but lives come out differently. All the bad things in the world flock to that point, like iron filings to a magnet, it forms a concentrated lump, a cyst. We are born uneasy and we die even more uneasy. It's not the fault of technology, of what man does to man; it's what goes on before, or above, or below. So whose fault is it? Are we chosen? Do we choose? A priest told me one day, 'A life like yours is a gift.' But what sort of a gift is it, I ask you? You go on, you hold out, you grit your teeth, for what?

Scientists have never done it, they've never done it but they should. They should work out why evil lights on those few places, just on those, always on the same ones. I think that beneath all this there's something like a chemical law, where elements are attracted to each other or repelled. That's why I'm saying they should take a look at it, find out what's happening and come up with some sort of antidote.

I can't sleep any more, I take pills but I still lie awake, the heat and the dust sweep in through the window, the geranium's still there, it's not alive and it's not dead. I've heard there are frogmen who go down into the sewers, they're paid thousands an hour, nobody's ever given me a penny, I toss and turn all night, I'm a diver too, the blankets are an underwater cave. It's dark, I go back and forth, I turn over, I'd like to get out but I can't work out which way is up, if the sky is still there where is it?

Nine o'clock already? You've got to go? Give me a kiss before you leave.

Look at these letters I still get, it's incredible isn't it? Fifteen years on and they still send them to me. Always the same printed card with the words, 'We have in our possession the following objects . . .' and they list all the things my daughter left over there. Once, ages ago, I even wrote back, I said thanks very much you keep them, it must have got lost or else they didn't understand my handwriting, over the years your writing changes, too, it starts to look like hens' scratchings. It's hot today, isn't it? It'll soon be the holidays, are you going some-where nice? No, I'm staying here, where would I go? I keep the shutters down, I've got a little fan, I put it on the table there where the teapot is, I watch television or rather I keep it on. Reading, no, I'm not interested. You read when you are curious and I'm not any more, since Serena died I've never got through a whole book. She used to devour them, yes, have you seen the other rooms? The books lining the walls are all hers, she started piling them up when she was still a girl. At one point she got it into her head that she wanted to be a writer. She loved thrillers. She used to cut out pieces of news from the papers and keep them in separate folders – a yellow one for rapes, a red one for murders – she was desperate to keep everything in order. She lived inside the murderer's skin, she breathed with his lungs, saw with his eyes, she looked for him everywhere, the stories she wrote got more and more complicated, sometimes they were so complicated you couldn't be sure who the dead man was any more, or at least I was never sure, she always said it was crystal clear. I wasn't happy about it right from the start, not the fact that she wrote stories but the fact that she took to lingering among dead bodies as if they were flowers. After a few years she started publishing, her books did well, so I said well maybe that's it, this is her talent, it's a job like any other, she could have been a doctor or a lawyer, she writes thrillers, it's just the same. But it always made me a bit anxious, if she'd seemed at peace perhaps I wouldn't have been so on edge but she always seemed restless. Being successful and writing those dreadful things didn't calm her down at all. It wasn't just a way of getting things out of her system, you see, something which as she did it would soothe her pain. No, she was hooked on it, she often muddled up her own life with her stories, she thought she was being followed along the road, she was afraid of opening cupboards. During her last years she said the biggest one's still inside me, deep down I have the perfect thriller. She had it but she couldn't bring it out, she would go off on one journey after another, she was getting worse all the time. I didn't try to advise her, I stayed silent, what could I say? When she told me she was leaving for America – she was going to New York for inspiration because there were stacks of crimes there – I said fine, you're doing the right thing.

A month later a cleaner found her in a lift. They never found out who strangled her.

In the papers they wrote that she'd died like one of her own characters. The police made some investigations. Why was she in that lift? What had she been doing that evening? The case was never closed. I don't care, do you know what I felt when they told me the news? It's dreadful, and I'm ashamed to say it, but I was pleased, pleased for her I mean, not for me. Does that make me a monster? That's life, you sow a seed, you watch the plant grow, you wait for it to be torn out by the root. Since I've been on my own I've wondered if maybe the Indians are right, souls move about, they go from here to there, they pay here for what they did there, if they've already paid they are happy . . . If that's the way it is, what must I have done in another life? It's something I think about a lot and it terrifies me. I think maybe I was a hyena, a hungry tiger, in a past life I scattered blood all around, I scattered it then and now it's being scattered all around me. What lesson should I have learned? There's a time to kill and a time to heal, there's a time to destroy and a time to build. I killed everything, destroyed everything, what did I ever build? A few thoughts which go round in circles, the nonsensical thoughts of a simpleton. Why is it I still go on, move, turn round, and still don't understand a thing? If there was a lesson, what was it? I shout out loud and nobody hears me, so I ask myself how do you let go, how can you have trust? Trust in what? I often feel so bitter, you know, bitter that I was never really good at anything. I never did anyone any harm, I never had the urge to, but harm has come crashing down on me like a cloudburst. So then I wonder, if I'd been the one to do harm first would I perhaps have been happier? And what then? Who can say anything about after? I don't see, I don't believe, I don't give a damn about scales, balances and accounts: this is where we play out our games, where we know, nowhere else. When Serena died, for a while I thought this is the final test, something will come down from the sky, a sense of calm and peace. But nothing came down, I stayed here in my armchair with my tiny, tiny thoughts, like little mice scurrying in their hole. But perhaps that's what it is, it's this smallness which has destroyed me. I never dared anything. The look in my eyes? Like a lamb before Easter, there I was with my eyes closed and the axe hanging over me, even though I couldn't see it I could feel the cold blade on my neck, that chill wind hanging in the air. If I had any talents I never used them, I went on in utter inertia, there was a wave bearing me along and there I was in the middle of it like an old shoe, a tin can, every day, all my life I've paddled backwards and forwards in the scum without ever getting anywhere. I've done no harm, I've done no good, I've done nothing.

Before you came today I picked up an old magazine. There was a long interview with an old philosopher – they always interview philosophers when they are about to die. He was talking about old age. He said that nature is full of goodness and foresight because there comes a point when everything gets blurred, you don't have strong emotions any more, your senses begin to fade, you hear less, you see less. Everything becomes as if shrouded in cotton wool, you are sailing on calm water, you see the coast line drift away, it gets and fainter and fainter ... it disappears and that's the end.

When I'd read that, do you know what I wanted to do? I wanted to write him a letter, then I looked at the date of the magazine and I didn't write it, it came out years ago, he must be dead by now. Anyway, if I had written, I would have written that he was making a big mistake. It's not true that everything drifts off into the distance or at least it's partly true, you hear less, you see less and you move less but instead of helping that just makes things more difficult. Smaller things become blurred, you have fewer distractions, and so the burning core emerges in all its dramatic intensity, it's there, burning away, licking at the foundations, and it is devastating. It's a lie that old people have no passions; they have terrible passions which are fed, bolstered, strengthened by their remorse. There's no point having any regrets, people should know that from the start, they should sing it to children in their cot along with their nursery rhymes, but nobody sings you that song so how are you supposed to know? By the time you realize, it's too late. You see? You're always back at the point you started, there's no way out.

So your legs are feeble, your eyes are dim, the only sounds you hear are low-pitched ones and suddenly you feel this desire in you, a mocking desire. You want to move, leave, take a long trip. You want to see new places, go back to places you've already seen. That's what happens as you prepare to leave this world.

I've travelled very little. Venice, Florence, the usual places. I only went further afield the once – Serena was

175

twelve years old – I went to Israel to see my father. He was an old man by then, I wanted her to get to know her only remaining grandparent.

She was going through an unbearable phase at the time, she had this obsession that she went on and on about all the time. Somebody, at school I suppose, had told her that Hitler wasn't dead, there was a body in the bunker but nobody could say for sure it was his. She already had a knack for thrillers, so she spent all her time coming up with different hypotheses, the ones she thought most likely were always the most dreadful ones. Shortly before the end he'd killed a man down there who was his spitting image. Perhaps he'd put the man together in a laboratory, cloned him the same way as you clone roses, he'd killed him and then escaped without ever coming back up to the surface. He'd escaped along underground passages which were there in place ever since he came to power. They'd been built by the best engineers in the land, they spread out like arteries under every part of the world, they came out in Australia and Indochina, Greenland and Chile. There were secret little doors for him to come out of.

Obviously there was food down there, water, everything he needed to survive. There were enough supplies for thousands of people because he wasn't going to be down there all alone, and he had that replicating machine with him. He'd crossed himself with bloodhounds, the best hunting bloodhounds. There were hundreds and thousands of them down there by now, there was hardly any room left in the passageways, they ran up and down and never got tired, they would sniff the air hungrily, any smells they would devour with their nose, as they breathed in they made a terrible noise. When the smell was the right one they would bare their teeth, they were wolves with their jaws open, ready to spring. They'd been living down there for twenty years, they were multiplying down there, they moved around in packs. They were just waiting for a whistle, a signal, something to let them know that the time had come again to wipe out impurity from the world.

You see? Serena lived with that fantasy in her head. For her it was much more than a fantasy, it was true. She would spend all her time washing herself, she would rub at her body so hard that her skin almost came away. She never stepped on manhole covers or on air vents in the pavement. Every evening she put a marble slab over the toilet. It had seemed a good idea, the best idea, to take her over there. That way she could get to know her granddad and she would realize there was a place where she could be safe. I told her that even if the wolves tried to get out they couldn't, there was a huge army ready and waiting just in case. I also told her that if she wanted, if it would make her feel any better, we could move over there. There was nothing to keep us in the city where we were living, it would have been easy to do.

In fact she did calm down a bit. She liked this grandfather of hers who was so out of this world; all he thought about was cows or playing his violin. They went on long walks together, up and down the fruit orchards. History for him was just a pale memory; he watched the plants growing, the calves coming on. His whole life was taken up that way, with nature. He was a happy man and for a while he managed to pass on some of his happiness to her. We spent a month together, absorbed into the peace of the kibbutz.

A week before coming home I decided to take a short trip to a few places nearby. I wanted to leave them alone for a bit, perhaps my absence would help Serena come to a decision. Taking just a single bag with me, I crossed over into Jordan. In Jerusalem I took a room in a small hotel near the Jaffa gate and for three days I wandered round aimlessly. Since my time in the convent it was the first time I found myself free of any tie, alone with myself. Now and then as I walked down the narrow streets, the cries of the muezzin ringing in my ears, I was overcome by a sense of unreality. The place was so filled with God that I could barely breathe. So I would sit on a low wall, place my hands on my legs and squeeze them. The next to last day I took a bus down to the Dead Sea.

That's what you don't expect when you leave Jerusalem, you don't expect that after the olive groves there is the desert, that terrible desert with nothing but rocks and bumps. As soon as the bus set off I started to feel uneasy. I was afraid of being there, alone in that heavy heat in a place where there was absolutely nothing. What would I do all day? I wanted to get off and go back but by then it was too late.

I left the bus close by the valley of the Song of Songs. You've been there too, I think. In the distance you could just make out the rock of Masada, like an enormous rampart. In front of it were those waters, still as glass.

I walked for a while along the water's edge, I took off my shoes, my stockings, I dipped my toes in. I could have gone right in but I was afraid those dead waters would suck me down, that they would burn up my heart and my eyes.

Walking and walking I lost all track of time. Over there, as you know, it gets dark very quickly, night comes down faster than a shop shutter. Only when all of a sudden shapes began to go fuzzy did I realize it was late, that I had to go back to the road and wait for the bus. I reached the bus stop and began waiting. I waited and waited. By now the sun was down and there was no sign of the bus. Totally absorbed in my own thoughts, I'd forgotten to check the bus timetable. There were no more buses and there weren't even any more cars going by. The few lights around soon went out, there was no one around. All of a sudden everything went still and double, like a Saturday. This really was the Sabbath.

Are you hot? Shall I switch on the fan? No? Open the window, then will you, let a bit of air in, it's stifling in here. Sit somewhere else though, otherwise you'll get a stiff neck.

What was I saying? The desert? Yes, there I was, all alone with my pockets empty. Even if I'd had money with me there were no hotels. I walked away from the road, I was afraid to sleep near it, you know how many people there are up to no good in every country. It was night but you could see perfectly clearly, the moon was full in the sky, its whiteness was spreading over the land, the sea, the sand, over the skeletal branches of the acacia-trees. Guided by that light, I turned into a small valley; there was a river running below and all around vegetation that was almost tropical. I should have been terrified – I had never slept out in the open air, in an unfamiliar place – I should have been scared but actually I was perfectly serene, I was even singing. I was singing that little song of my mother's about the bees, I liked the idea that nobody knew where I was, it gave me a kind of exaltation. I thought, I could die and that made me happy . . . It would have been a marvellous death. When I found a sheltered spot, I lay down. The sand was still hot from the sun, it was a warm blanket, the stars were out . . .

There I was in the middle, a little eddy in the midst of other whirlpools. I lay down on my back, looking up. Before falling asleep I watched the night sky for a long time – something else I'd never done before – I watched it and was sorry I didn't know the names of the stars. For me, as for the majority of human beings, they were all the same, just accessories. Yes, suddenly I would like to have been able to call them as if in a rollcall – Sirius, Orion, Centaur . . . suddenly an odd idea popped into my head, I thought my mother and Bruno were sitting up there, astride a star. If I'd known the names I could have called them down, talked with them for a long time as I'd never been able to do while they were still alive . . . The Sabbath had come round again, you see, once again I was seeing everything with double eyes, there were the things as they appeared and as they were really, all mixed in together as you looked at them. You could hear the jackals around, the small rustling sounds of night – that's when the desert comes alive – there were all these strange noises but I still wasn't afraid. Before falling asleep I thought of Jonah the rebel. The Leviathan who swallowed him had swallowed me down, too. There I'd been since the day I was born, bobbing about amongst the trivial plankton. When he sank down into the depths I was flapping about inside him, a blind and restless tadpole . . . There I was cursing, thrashing about . . . And I was so caught up that I hadn't noticed the monster had opened his jaws, he was rising up to the surface and opening them wide to catch fish. He swallowed fish and air along with them. Shards of light came flooding in and lit up his gullet, his trachea, his oesophagus. It would have lit me up, too, if I had been paying more attention, if I had seen it.

That's what I thought as I fell asleep.

At dawn the light came up shining and bright, it rose with a slow caress – I opened my eyes and I said to myself, light doesn't strike, it caresses – the light was caressing everything and the breeze was getting up. It's a wind that lasts hardly any time at all, by the time the sun is up it's already died down. I was lying there on the ground, in the middle of all this light and this breeze, I was no longer an eddy amongst the whirlpools but wind among wind, air, breath. I was no longer anything. I had no desire to get up or to walk on. I stayed there while things changed from silhouettes to shapes . . . And just as I was lying there, without moving, I felt it: I was still but the earth was moving beneath me, backwards and forwards in a regular, rocking movement. For a moment I thought it was an earthquake, but it was an idea I soon dismissed: if it had been that, the trees would have been moving too, the movement would have got stronger and stronger and shaken everything. Then I listened some more, I stretched out my full length to hear better and after a while I understood. I understood it in that fraction of a second and I've never understood it since. I don't know whether to tell you or not, I'm afraid that when you leave here you'll just laugh, you'll go off thinking poor old soul, but it's not that, really, try to listen to what I'm saying. It was the Sabbath.

The earth breathes. With us up above, it breathes its quiet breathing.